INTO THE
ABYSS

Born and raised in New Delhi, **Ayush Ansal** is an author with a passion for the darker aspects of literature. While enjoying authors such as Mario Puzo and Agatha Christie at a younger age, he currently favours classics such as the works of Edgar Allan Poe and H.P. Lovecraft. He studied at Modern School Vasant Vihar and The British School in New Delhi before moving to Gordonstoun School in Scotland. He is currently in his second year at the Warwick Business School in England.

In addition to his higher education, Ayush spends his summers interning and working. Looking towards the future, he aspires to enter the business environment and dynamic corporate landscape of the new generation.

INTO THE
ABYSS

AYUSH ANSAL

RUPA

Published by
Rupa Publications India Pvt. Ltd 2016
7/16, Ansari Road, Daryaganj
New Delhi 110002

Sales centres:
Allahabad Bengaluru Chennai
Hyderabad Jaipur Kathmandu
Kolkata Mumbai

Copyright © Ayush Ansal 2016

This is a work of fiction. Names, characters, places and incidents are either the product of the author's imagination or are used fictitiously and any resemblance to any actual person, living or dead, events or locales is entirely coincidental.

All rights reserved.
No part of this publication may be reproduced, transmitted, or stored in a retrieval system, in any form or by any means, electronic, mechanical, photocopying, recording or otherwise, without the prior permission of the publisher.

ISBN: 978-81-291-3958-0

First impression 2016

10 9 8 7 6 5 4 3 2 1

The moral right of the author has been asserted.

Printed by Replika Press Pvt. Ltd, India

This book is sold subject to the condition that it shall not, by way of trade or otherwise, be lent, resold, hired out, or otherwise circulated, without the publisher's prior consent, in any form of binding or cover other than that in which it is published.

To my father and grandfather

*Beneath the pressure of torments such as these,
the feeble remnant of the good within me succumbed.*
~EDGAR ALLAN POE , *The Black Cat*

contents

Prologue /xi

The Fall of Harry Winterfield / 1

The Frivolity of Harvey Hyde / 29

The Sacrifice of Jin Hanzo / 55

The Ballad of Amy Burrows / 89

The Paranoia of Richard Fern / 109

The Generosity of Ken Kitano / 119

The Ambition of Sam Winterfield / 147

The Loyalty of Fasial Haseem / 161

The Retribution of David Darlington / 183

prologue

Resting on the southern fringe of the United Kingdom, Portsmouth was as a thriving settlement, having historically existed in a grey limbo. Such was the case as perhaps it was without the enthralling enthusiasm that drives light within the void of collective humanity. On the south-west corner of this commune, in close proximity to the infamous Portsmouth historical dockyard, a hub of travel found itself with the appellation of the Portsmouth Harbour rail station.

With his feet resting on the cold stone floor of Platform 2 and his swift eyes watching the men and women who walked towards him from the Wight Link ferry terminal that was on the opposite end of the structure, a man in a long black overcoat stood within the crowd, hiding in the crowd and basking in its anonymity. His physical structure, while concealed by the dark colours of his apparel, was not extraordinary. He was thin but not weak and his height was average and unassuming. His face was concealed by a fedora which hung low over his face. If one aimed to truly unmask him, they would perhaps stare at his countenance with repeated failures, only to be encouraged by his cracked smile that came alive as a disjointed sight in our crumbling reality.

He heard gentle footsteps approaching him, but his unchanging being failed to display any indication that he had been awaiting them. But he had watched closely the face that walked towards him, a cold unblinking stare had greeted the arrival, but a tone of formality and the weight of the uncut atmosphere hung heavily upon them.

The Old Man, still draped in his dark overcoat and concealing fedora, studied the individual across from him. They were cut from the same cloth and he could feel the synergy of their unnerving and disquieting actuality. The other man was much younger and perhaps physically stronger. He wore a black pinstripe suit, which was polished and cut from the finest fabrics. His countenance was rugged and the rounded cigar leaning from the corner of his mouth suggested that his youngish being but ageing extremities were a victim of his habits.

The cigar smoking gentleman, a stretch of the imagination to label him so, leaned in close to the Old Man that stood across from him and whispered with familiarity and similarity in his ear. It seemed uncertain and the fibre of the event certainly seemed to lack commonality as the Old Man, whose lethal nature was far from lacking, allowed the man in the pinstripe suit to grace the closest boundaries of his personal proximity and listened closely as the words were whispered in his ear, 'Winterfield knows.'

The Fall of Harry Winterfield

one

Two men sat in a small white office cabin, uncomfortably watching each other.

The resident of the office, Richard Fern, was forty-six years old and a middle manager at the Boxler Banking Institution (which had come to be more commonly known as the BBI). He was skinny and frail, with thick black hair with white streaks. He was wearing an expensive suit, but looked worse for wear.

Palmer Tubb, a chubby contractor who was younger than the bank manager but looked older due to his overweight body and balding head, sat across him. He was sweating profusely as the tension in the room thickened and the silence was filled by the ticking clock and gentle breeze that blew outside.

'I sincerely hope you're wrong,' said Fern.

'I sincerely hope so too,' agreed Tubb.

'So let's go over this again. I want to see if we've missed anything...' began Fern. 'Two days ago, you returned to the construction site after hours, to retrieve your wallet which you thought you had left in your office...'

'Well, it was actually just a day ago because it was after midnight,' interrupted Tubb.

'Whatever. Then you headed back to the site, at which point you discovered two black cars parked outside the Sector E buildings. That's between Towers 47 and 48, right?'

'Yeah, those are the ones that we've just started working on.'

'What kind of cars were they?'

'Expensive. Two black BMWs, I think.'

'So you saw the cars, realized they weren't meant to be there since the site had closed for the night, and then pulled up near them and headed into Sector E to investigate?'

'Yeah, I mean I wrote down the license plate numbers, but I seem to have lost the paper.'

'You lost the paper?' Fern asked, his voice growing stern.

'Yeah, I'm sorry,' Tubb replied, looking down.

'Those plate numbers would have be really helpful. Are you sure you can't recall where you might've put the paper?'

'I've looked for it everywhere. I have no idea where it is.'

'Well, that's a shame. So, you headed into Sector E and saw Winterfield and two other men. Describe what happened after that.'

'Well, I walked into Sector E. You know that section is completely walled up, so you can't see anything from outside. I entered through the main entrance. They must have heard me because they turned around as soon I stepped in. I recognized our boss, Mr Winterfield, with two men in black suits. I'm quite sure that one of them was Hugh Rudy, the structural engineer from Winterfield Estates. I didn't know the other man though.'

'How did they react to you walking in on them?'

'As soon as they saw me, the other man pulled out a

revolver and asked me to leave. I wasn't planning on arguing with a man holding a gun. So I left, drove home and then called you.'

'What were they doing there, Tubb?'

'Well there was a hole in one of the structural pillars, which was reported earlier. It seemed as though Rudy had paid a visit to check the strength of the support structure. He only needs to look at the issue once to realize what we'd been up to.'

Richard leaned back in his chair. Understanding the incident in detail only made him feel worse. A shadow of gloom passed over his face.

two

IN HIS LARGE London office on the top floor of his building, Chairman of the Board Harry Winterfield stood staring down at the Thames from his bulletproof wall-sized window. His cliché-but-modern office with minimalist furniture and excessive use of white bored him. He stood lost in thought even though a man, Calvin, stood near the couch.

'Pour me a glass of Dom, Calvin,' Winterfield said.

The young man, with misleadingly innocent face, hesitated, 'Dom Perignon, Sir? I didn't realize we were celebrating today.'

'At my age, I can't wait for a special occasion to enjoy what I love.'

Calvin approached the tiny bar cabinet in the office and popped-open the bottle. He nervously poured a single glass and served it to his boss.

Winterfield took a sip of the bubbly. He was glad he had worked hard enough to treat himself to luxuries such as these, as and when he pleased.

'We've been mucked around with, Calvin. And as someone who has pushed around a lot of people in his life, I can tell you that it is really upsetting when the hunter becomes the prey.'

'Has something happened, Sir?' asked the young man, curiously.

'Tell me what you know about our SkyStar Project.'

Calvin raced his mind. This could be a test or maybe just a simple question but he didn't know how the Boss operated, no one did.

'It's a 200 acre project being developed by us on the northern border of the Outer London boroughs. We're building fifty luxury towers, thirty stories each.'

'Ah, good job, my boy. But you forgot to mention one thing.'

'What's that, Sir?'

'It's going to be the greatest loss-making venture in the history of Winterfield Estates.'

three

A SMALL, BRONZE PUB located near Victoria Station, The Wicked & Wise, usually saw its largest influx of customers at around 5.15 p.m. from Monday to Friday. Only a five-minute walk from the main offices of Winterfield Estates, the pub was a popular choice for all the mid- to low-level employees of the company, marketing men and engineers alike.

The establishment was owned by an aging old Swede named Solomon, and had lately bloomed into a culturally significant part of the neighbourhood. Originally designed by the Russian Ivanovich family in the late 1800s, the pub carried an exquisitely ancient design that fit well into its posh surroundings.

On a small table outside the pub, four lawyers from the firm's legal department sat with pints in one hand and cigarettes in the other sharing a bowl of fries. Calvin was sitting with his friends, with every eye turned towards him. He often inspired jealousy among his three friends as he was the boss's hand-picked protégé.

The other three were Albert, Bruno and Darwin. All three bore some similarities—slightly chubby but with clean, polished and handsome faces and neat hair. From a distance, they could easily be mistaken for one another, though after a closer inspection and time spent with them, Bruno stood out a little with his obtrusively strong Scottish accent. Calvin found that he stood out the most as he was both shorter and skinnier than the other three, not to mention bronze-skinned in contrast to their pale complexion.

'So Albert tells me that you've found out the truth,' Darwin said to Calvin, after taking a drag from his cigarette.

'Susie Q' by Creedence Clearwater Revival came on the jukebox.

'He has! But he said he wouldn't tell us until we were all together after work,' added Albert.

'What on earth are you boys talking about?' asked Bruno.

Darwin turned to Bruno and answered, 'Ah, we forgot you weren't a part of this. That's what you get for being on a different floor.'

'The view is nicer!' defended Bruno.

'Anyway…' continued Darwin, 'Well, there's this man who visits the boss occasionally. Nobody really knows who he is. He's this skinny, scrawny fellow who always wears this long black trench coat.'

'It's an overcoat,' corrected Albert

Darwin explained further, 'Yeah, an overcoat. He also wears this black hat. Like those old gangsters from the 20s used to wear. He pulls it over his face.'

'A fedora?' chipped in Bruno.

Darwin continued, 'So, he comes into our office about once a month wearing this long black overcoat and this fedora pulled over his face, and he walks straight into the boss's office without even speaking to his secretary. It's all very mysterious.'

'So we had a bet,' said Albert, 'I said that he was probably a friend of Winterfield. Darwin claimed that he was from the London Mob and Winterfield was being shaken down, while Calvin proposed that he was probably a personal investigator that the boss had hired.'

Bruno weighed in, 'This man sounds more like a bag man to me. The kind of person whose job it is to deliver cash bribes to or from Winterfield. Did he ever have a bag or a briefcase on him?'

'No bag, no briefcase of any sort,' stated Darwin.

'Maybe he hid the money in his coat?' Bruno wondered aloud.

'Look, it doesn't matter anymore. Calvin is here to tell us who he actually is,' Albert interrupted.

The three men turned to Calvin. He took a deep breath.

He put down his pint of Cider and said, 'Well, he's not a private investigator, which is quite disappointing; he definitely had that look.'

'As I've said before, there is no such thing as a private investigator look,' said Darwin.

'Yes, there is!' argued Calvin. 'Well, anyway I was speaking to Winterfield today, and he told me that the man in the overcoat is a consultant.'

'A consultant? A consultant for what?' asked Bruno.

'SkyStar. We don't usually do much luxury work so the boss wanted to bring in a specialist. And that man in the overcoat is that specialist,' Calvin clarified.

'That's all?' Darwin asked feeling let down.

'That's all,' said Calvin.

four

EIGHT YEARS AGO, Harry Winterfield had pulled every string possible and used every contact he had in the real estate market to purchase his house. The mansion was originally a church that was being sold as a historical monument, but the size of the plot was good so he bought it. It took over a year to procure the license to allow residential developments and have the church demolished. While it burnt a deep hole into the pockets of the blossoming Winterfield family, the Church of England saw its donation boxes flooded with money. Many guessed it to be buyer's guilt, but the truth was that Harry Winterfield was simply a god-fearing man with a skewed view on ethics.

The Victorian-style mansion itself was grossly oversized for the family of three. The architecture and the dark interiors and furnishings made it seem almost gothic.

The brooding walls forebode a sense of impending nothingness and its residents were often consumed with strange and drowning thoughts. Such was perhaps the effect of the interiors themselves, or perhaps it was nothing more than a psychosomatic symptom of the intense emptiness of space that stimulated a lonely mind.

Linda Winterfield had married into money. She was unaware whether her husband's work was conventional and appreciated or not but she didn't care. She was just glad she was comfortable and had her young son, Sam, to look after.

Their son was only ten years old and so he didn't fully comprehend the raw power of wealth that his father had displayed in buying a mansion in the middle of London. Everyone else did though, and there was no shortage of newspaper articles about it too, mostly supportive. The Winterfields had given too much to too many people to have their reputation or intentions questioned.

Sitting in his home office in a green Victorian chair facing a huge Victorian table to match, Harry Winterfield flipped through the pages of the latest *The Economist*, when the phone on his desk rang.

'Hello, who is this?' asked Mr Winterfield, as his phone flashed an unknown number.

'Mr Winterfield, it's Harvey Hyde speaking,' the voice said, urgently.

'Ah yes, Mr Hyde. What can I do for you?'

'Sir, there seems to a discrepancy that needs to be resolved urgently. When and where would be the earliest you can meet?'

In moment's silence, Harry realized the gravity of the matter. Real estate was a slow business market, which usually takes months and years to develop. To request an instantaneous meeting was an exceptionally rare occasion and one that reflected an unusually serious problem.

'Come to the Croquet Lounge in 45 minutes.'

five

By charging an exorbitantly large amount as the annual fee, the Croquet Lounge had become popular because it guaranteed that each of its members was rich enough to afford a discreet place to carry out their clandestine business.

One could say that the establishment maintained a royal clientele, and an atmosphere soaked in the delicacies of legendary tenures and the greatness of men. Industries had been altered and futures had been menaced and curated within the very walls where members now sat.

The Lounge offered no facilities other than allowing indoor smoking and an open bar. There was no actual Croquet facility on site, just a collection of ultra-luxurious furniture placed around in a large room with expensive carpeting accompanied by wooden walls and ceilings. There were no waiters trampling around on the carpet so there was no risk of being overheard. Furthermore, the bartender was the owner of the lounge itself and was deaf, understanding his patron's orders by lip-reading. The Croquet Lounge was also a tax-free establishment, half of all earnings were donated to charities dedicated to supporting war veterans.

Harry Winterfield sat on a sofa in the back of the

lounge. In front of him was a bottle of Dom Perignon and a glass. Both of which he had carried from the bar himself. He was wearing a beige suit with a white shirt and a red tie. Nothing extraordinary, except for the fact that he was wearing something very expensive, but it was probably one of the cheapest pieces of clothing compared to what the rest of the patrons were wearing.

Harvey Hyde entered the establishment. Strong-jawed and headstrong as always, he briskly paced towards Winterfield and shook his hand upon reaching him and then took a seat across him.

'What's wrong Hyde?' asked the older man. He had learned that respecting one's subordinates was a severely undervalued tool.

'Dom Perignon, Sir? It seems eccentric to be celebrating in such a trying time like this.'

'I'm not celebrating. I just like a bit of Dom.'

'Why not live the good life every day when one can afford it?'

Mr Winterfield ignored the rhetoric question and got to the point, 'What's the problem, Hyde?'

'Well Sir, it's regarding SkyStar. It's the first time we're doing luxury work and someone seems to be taking advantage.'

'Don't be vague.'

'I first came across the problem four days ago on the 12th of this month. I was doing my efficiency audits as usual when I noticed a severe discrepancy. If we consider Tower 5, we had initially decided to spend £100,000 per floor for the framework and that's how much money has been allocated. However, a substandard structure costing only £60,000 has been developed, which will barely hold up the building and probably collapse under a luxury build. Not to mention the quality is much below the standard we got approved from the Government.'

'So someone's been stealing £40,000 from us per floor per building?'

'Basically, a severe case of embezzlement, yes.'

'And how much is that in total?'

'Sixty million pounds, Sir. Enough to punch a serious hole in our cash flow.'

'To hell with the cash flow, Hyde. No one steals from me. I need to be sure, however. I want to see the structure quality myself.'

'We could do that next week, Sir.'

'We're going now.'

Both men got up. Winterfield finished his glass of champagne and then chugged a little from the bottle. He called Hugh Rudy, his most trustworthy structural engineer and asked him to meet at the site.

six

WINTERFIELD STOOD STARING at the hole that Hugh Rudy had just made in the wall. It was only a foot in a diameter but the process had been enough to severely disrupt his thinking.

Behind him, he heard Hyde bark the word, 'Leave.'

Thinking he was talking to him, Winterfield quickly turned around to see Hyde aiming a small revolver at the contractor Tubb. The chubby man had quickly backed away, as any sensible person would, and after hearing Tubb's car drive away, Hyde holstered the revolver.

The engineer wondered if it was commonplace to carry a gun in this town and if he is putting himself at a disadvantage by not carrying one. The boss clearly realized that carrying a concealed weapon often attracted more danger than it could be used to deal with.

Hyde turned to his boss's uneasy gaze. He however didn't realize that these two men were highly uncomfortable around weapons and simply smiled at them in return.

'What kind of revolver is that?' asked Winterfield, trying to regain control of the situation.

Hyde once again drew out the gun, but this time only to check for the model.

Seeing it up close, Rudy realized that the gun wasn't just a simple revolver, but more like an oversized hand-cannon with an intimidating barrel length.

'It's a Smith & Wesson Model 500,' he remarked from memory, unable to find any notable marking. His face suggested that he was impressed with himself.

Winterfield took a breath and asked carefully, 'Well, Hyde, was it really necessary to aim your Smith & Wesson Model 500 at out chubby old Tubb? He could've just come down here to check up on us. It's his job to look after all parts of the site, including the security.'

'Sir, he really should have been more focused on looking after his own security because there is a decent chance that I would've blown his head off if I didn't have you two here as witnesses,' Hyde remarked calmly.

'And why would you have killed him?' asked Winterfield in what seemed like an insane line of questioning to Hugh Rudy.

'Because, Sir...' began Hyde. 'As an Efficiency Auditor for Winterfield Real Estates, I aim to help the company be successful and that aim of mine is severely obstructed if contractors like him are managing to steal sums the size of 60 million pounds from the company.'

'You think that good old Tubb is this master thief?' asked Hugh Rudy laughingly.

'Well obviously, he's not alone. He's not smart or ballsy enough to do this by himself. But he's certainly part of it. Only the contractor controls what materials are actually used in construction,' Hyde explained quickly.

Winterfield considered the situation gravely but knew that he had an even more immediate problem at hand.

'Is that gun legal?' he asked Hyde.
The efficiency auditor chuckled.
'Where'd you get it then?' asked Winterfield curiously.
Hyde smiled sinfully and replied, 'I know a guy.'

seven

THE MAN IN the overcoat sat across from Richard Fern. They sat on two lawn chairs that had been frequented by the man whenever he wanted a truly safe conversation or a cigar to himself. It was his private office in the open. They stared at the view across them; a sight of beauty to some, a boring industrial setting to others. Hundreds of containers were constantly being loaded and unloaded from ships. Nothing could be heard because of the distance, but the sheer size of the operation was clearly visible.

This was the second time Fern had met this man. He had been as mysterious the first time but the banker could easily say he knew more about the man's real identity than most did.

To everyone in London, the frail man with the tipped fedora and long black overcoat was Quintin Stonewall—a consultant for many things, but all expensive things. He was almost like a royalty dealer to the city, pointing wealthy men in the direction of how their vast wealth was best expended. These propositions could be for private frivolity or business prestige. Yet, his origin was vague and his history unknown.

His real identity, as learned by Fern after spending an exorbitant amount of the Boxler Banking Institution's money in information shops, was that of Faisal Haseem, a fair skinned half-Arab that had worked for an Arab dictator for nearly a decade. He had been a commander of the secret police, known by the common folk as the 'Handyman' due to his ability to strangle his victims to death with his bare hands. After the dictator had been toppled by British forces, Faisal had been 'rescued' as a part of a ploy to convince Her Majesty's government that he was in fact a dictator's prisoner and was an architect exploited for his knowledge on Victorian Architecture and how to create buildings of similar grandeur in. Granted unlimited asylum in the UK, Faisal had begun conquering the weak and enthralling the wealthy in the guise of an aging Englishman with a passion for mysterious dark clothing.

Usually operating through espionage and anonymity to maintain his multiple personas in corporate London, Faisal consented for the occasional meeting with Fern. The money they were going to make together dwarfed his other interests.

The banker knew that Faisal could be trusted with sensitive information as he would hold his silence for an infinite amount of time.

'Winterfield is still ignorant. So everything's going according to plan.'

The Old Man let out a soft grunt. His pitch black fedora tipped even lower across his face.

'How's Tubby?'

'Palmer Tubb?' chuckled Fern, 'He's unreliable, naïve and a downright liability. But he's the contractor so we're stuck with him.'

The Old Man didn't reply. He simply continued to quietly

watch the containers being lifted and buried.

Fern continued, 'It's looking good though. No one really doubts the work so we'll have more of the cash in hand quite soon. I hope you can manage to convince Winterfield to spend even more. It'll increase our cut. You're a wise man; I hope you can influence him.'

'He'll query about funds.' The Old Man mused.

'Reassure him that my bank can and will double the investment, if need be. I'll make it happen. We need to maximize our take here. There's a good chance we won't be welcome in London afterwards.' Richard spoke coldly. They were playing the big game here. But he was not as aware of the reality as the Old Man.

The Old Man had seen men beg, suffer and die for a whole lot less. He saw it as a blessing to be situated in a land of such luxury where innocence seemed to prevail and every devious soldier ever caught was painted as the devil. However, he wanted to break the system, to own the souls of those around him and rule from within. He wanted the power in his hand and only vast sums of money could hold the world hostage the way he wanted to. Was it his bitterness that had unleashed this desire within him? Unlikely. It was just that he was afraid. The kind of fear that grew when no number of safety nets could protect him from those he had buried beneath him.

eight

𝒟ECADES AGO, FAISAL Haseem had begun to cultivate himself as a ruthless man.

'Do you wish to suffer?' asked Faisal calmly.

The dictator was only and always referred to as The Shah. In his palace, the Shah had ordered the construction of a dungeon for his more nefarious practices. On this day, Faisal was using his position as the Commander of the Secret Police to conduct business in the facility under orders from his master.

A man across him, hung upside down, and was sweating and bleeding. His moans were muffled by his punctured lung.

Faisal crouched down and looked his victim in the eye. He leaned in closer and whispered, 'Always remember to enjoy the little things in life.'

nine

Sam Winterfield was an innocent boy living the life of a typical ten year old, albeit with the support of his rather successful parents. Young students did not choose to or want to think about why most of them walked home or went home by bus, while young Sam Winterfield was picked up in an expensive car.

Alone in his backyard, Sam lay on the grass staring up at the clouds and listening to songs on his portable radio. He enjoyed the weather and loved to spot shapes in the clouds. The radio played The Beatles and The Kinks, a classics marathon the host had called it. Not that Sam cared; he enjoyed most songs and was still at the age where he found it difficult to differentiate between generations of music.

He looked at his watch, it was still early in the afternoon, and he had a few hours before it was time for television. His friends spent their afternoons doing something known as chores. He never knew what that meant and wondered if he should be jealous of them as they seemed to have a routine way to pass the time.

His mother's voice cut across to him, interrupting his thoughts. It seemed she was shouting for him.

He jumped up and started walking towards the house.
His mother shouted again, 'Sam! Run!'
Sam ran. Not away from the house, but towards it.
Sam burst through the door and was faced with a sight that would haunt him forever.

His father Harry Winterfield was on his knees. Above him stood a man in a long black overcoat and a fedora pulled down over his face. The Old Man's, hands were wrapped around Harry Winterfield's neck. The suffocating man struggled for control. He was in rare situation of lacking the ability to alter his environment—he was being felled by a singular force—and the sinking expression on his face conveyed that honestly. Further at the end of the room, Linda Winterfield was being held back by a knife that had been driven through her thigh and into the wooden wall behind her.

Blood continued to run down his mother's leg. Her screams were drowned in the blood thumping in Sam's ears and his brain simply could not process the situation.

Eventually, when Harry had no life left in him at all, the Old Man let out a satisfied breath as his victim slumped to the floor. Sam then watched with continued horror as the Old Man smiled at him. Only his pristine white teeth were visible under his Fedora. His skin was wrinkled, and one could only suppose how such a frail creature possessed such immense strength.

The Old Man then approached Sam's mother. She didn't seem to have as much fight in her as her husband. He gripped her throat and squeezed it with a single hand. It was mere seconds before he felt her go cold in his hand. Her body dropped to the floor with a loud thud.

Sam stood silently. He trembled with fear as the Old Man walked slowly towards the young boy.

As he stepped close, he dropped to his knee and looked the boy in the eye. Sam stared into the horror itself, still frozen stiff as his brain did its best to not be crippled by the trauma.

The Old Man smiled at the boy and spoke coldly, 'It will seem unfair and I will be a horror. You will not understand why, but you must accept that it simply is. I do not expect you to forgive me nor do I ask for your forgiveness. There is no balance in this world, no justice. As time will pass, your memory will fade but your anger will grow. When the time finally comes, I will be at the end of your road awaiting your vengeance.'

Leaving him with those words, Sam watched his monster disappear.

ten

'I DON'T REMEMBER agreeing to murder,' Palmer Tubb exclaimed with worry.

He sat in the office of Richard Fern. In both their hands was a copy of the morning's newspaper, with the murder of Harry Winterfield and his wife as its headline.

'Well, what makes you think it had anything to do with you or me?' Fern was seriously hoping that the contractor would abandon this line of questioning. He knew the Old Man wouldn't hesitate in delivering the same fate to any other person.

Unfortunately, Tubb went down a dangerous road, 'You shared with me the real identity of our third partner, the consultant. This is his work, it's quite clear. Even so, Winterfield discovers our scam and the next day he's dead? That is no coincidence.'

A silence filled the room. Both men were painfully aware of the situation.

'Did Faisal consult with you on this?' asked Tubb after a few minutes.

Fern shook his head and replied, 'I just sent him a message telling him that Winterfield knows. He acted on his own after that.'

'So Faisal doesn't know that the Efficiency Auditor and the Structural Engineer are also aware of the situation?'

'Apparently not. If he did, that would just be two more deaths in the papers.'

'Should we tell him?'

'That will basically translate to us killing them, now that we know how Faisal will behave. I'm not sure if I can live with murder on my conscience.'

'I never agreed to murder but if there's a risk of going to prison instead, I may be easily convinced.'

'You know they have a son.'

'Who?'

'The Winterfields. It's not mentioned in the papers, but there's a ten year old boy, Sam. They've made an effort to keep his name out of the articles. Poor kid, orphaned at such a young age.'

'I feel guiltier now. Who's going to look after him?'

'An aunt or an uncle? Maybe grandparents? There'll be a long line of people willing to adopt a kid with that much wealth.'

'Maybe there's an opportunity here.'

'Don't act like filth. Very few people sink that low.'

'Yeah, I guess you're right. We need to focus on dealing with Mr Hyde and Mr Rudy anyway.'

'That's the Efficiency Auditor and the Engineer right?'

'Right, maybe we should pull them in? Offer them a cut?'

'That'll be a couple of million less for us each. It'll definitely be easier to just mention them to Faisal instead.'

'I guess we've got to do some thinking.'

The Frivolity of Harvey Hyde

one

Betwixt his birth and his confrontation with the contractor at SkyStar, Harvey Hyde found himself in a locale usually occupied by those who command much intellectual dexterity. An unusual name and an unusual establishment, The Pink Gentleman was a lounge for business, and business only. Nothing about the interiors of the lounge was actually pink. In any case, Dubai was well regarded as a tasteful city and such colouring would not have been accepted by the patrons. It was a small lounge with several large rooms. Each was big enough to seat groups of individuals all having their private meetings. In the Peacock Room, Hyde sat comfortably on a sofa at the far end. Two men were sitting across him.

A bottle of Bollinger lay on the table with only one glass out. The hosts of Hyde had refused to join him. He hadn't pushed too hard for them to have a glass, relishing the fact that he had the whole bottle to himself.

The two men across him were traditional Arabs with whom Hyde had repeatedly tried to get an appointment. After some perseverance, they had finally relented. The one to the right was Hussein Malik, a handsome man and the oldest son of the Malik family. In Dubai, the Malik family was almost considered to be royalty. The man on the left was his bodyguard. Forever silent, he could be relied on to never repeat any word he had ever heard to anyone else.

Hyde had requested to meet with Malik because the Malik family's recent investments in an iron mine had not gone too smoothly and seeing the opportunity, Hyde had offered his consulting services as an Efficiency Auditor, hoping to expand his horizons past Winterfield Estates.

'What makes you think you are the best person to audit our iron mines?' Hussein asked coldly.

'Sir, I am the best person to audit your mine for the same reason that this man is the best person to be your bodyguard. I am trustworthy and hard-working,' Hyde answered, as he sipped his Bollinger.

'Your words carry no weight with me,' Hussein stated bluntly.

'The current company I am working with, Winterfield Estates, has seen a 4 per cent rise in efficiency since I started looking at their projects. Those are solid results.'

'Four per cent improvement per month wouldn't be enough for me. You're not making a strong impression, Hyde.'

'Sir, that's where you notice a discrepancy,' retorted Hyde, trying to be as charming as he could, 'Winterfield Estates doesn't need an Efficiency Auditor with my skill. It's a booming company. The results I can provide are limited. But a failing venture, like your mine however? Well that's my dream situation. It's got the one thing I want.'

'And what is that one thing, Hyde? Money?' Hussein asked.

'No, Malik. It's potential,' Harvey leaned back having made his case.

Hussein Malik seemed impressed. However, their meeting was interrupted by a young girl who approached their table and handed Hussein his phone.

'You had left it in the car,' she whispered lovingly before leaving the men.

She had been at the table for a mere three seconds but that had been enough for Hyde to develop a sincere infatuation with her. Perfectly bronzed skin, flowing black hair, a slender figure and a gorgeous face. His jaw had widened, his eyes affixed, and his knees had trembled.

His words however were not as elegant. He turned to Hussein Malik and asked, 'Who is that gorgeous piece of meat? If she's your secretary or something, do you mind sending her over?'

The bodyguard's face burned with rage. Malik grimaced, clenching his knuckles. He announced sharply, 'That's my youngest sister, the princess of Dubai.'

Hyde had gravely insulted one of the most powerful men in the Arab world.

two

Lucy's Fish & Chips rested in one of the unpopular Edinburgh corridors that branched off from the main high street. It had an unappealing entrance, with a boring old sign that had the name of the shop printed in a yellow, almost unintelligible, font across a sea-blue background. This deterred anyone from walking in and encouraged them to resist the delightful smell of food that came from inside.

The interiors of the shop were as pale as ever with cheap boring white tiling, a blue counter and the classic old menu peeling off the wall. There was some place to sit inside on plastic chairs and tables; but a big bold sign that read 'Take-Out Encouraged' almost perfectly captured the mood of the shop.

Lucy was a sweet young lady, probably in her late 20s, with a quiet demeanour. She may have been better suited to working in a library or at a university but she couldn't complain as she had come to own an establishment of her own at quite a young age.

Wearing her blue self-made uniform, she was standing behind the counter and trying to solve a Sudoku puzzle in the newspaper. She looked behind to see that her chef was still dozing on her little plastic chair. Lucy's chef Hilda was an old lady that had agreed to work with her for astonishingly low pay. The two had met when Lucy was attending school in the city and Hilda had been the lunch-lady. The Principal had gotten lucky by hiring rotten-looking but now-notoriously talented Hilda to run the kitchen and maintain the minimum health standard. In all of Scotland, Lucy's school was the only one that never seemed to complain about the food.

At first, Lucy hadn't even considered an alternative for a chef. She had managed to hire dear old Hilda for nothing more than a slight increase in pay (as compared to the minimum wage that the school was paying her) and the sweetest pep-talk.

Was Lucy pretty? Maybe on the days she dressed up to go out on the town with her old friends. But on other days where her focus was making her cash-flow add up and ensuring the quickest service, she was boring. Not ugly or unattractive, simply plain and better suited to the background.

Despite the holiday season, unsurprisingly, it had been a quiet day. Lucy and Hilda had decided to keep the shop open anyway. Neither had any family to celebrate Christmas with, and the companionship was mutually appreciated.

The day was pleasant, if not mundane, but the peace was shattered by a loud bang in their alley. Hilda immediately woke up and grabbed a nearby pan. Two pairs of footsteps could be heard, both moving speedily in the direction of their shop.

A man burst into the shop. He was panting and clearly out of breath. Sweat dripped from his forehead. He did not bother to wipe it but instead simply charged towards Lucy and hopped over the counter, hiding himself on the other side right next to Lucy, his eyes closed and his face consumed with fear. Both Hilda and Lucy stood motionless, weary of the new stranger.

The doors to the shop burst open once again and a big hulking bronze-skinned man walked in. He was dressed in an expensive suit and his square-jawed face had a level of polish that was intimidating. He was handsome in the traditional sense but the rage that consumed his countenance gently masked that.

'Where is he?' he asked Lucy with a strong accent.

Lucy stood silently not knowing whether or not to protect the man trembling at her feet.

Hilda and Lucy simply stared at the intruder.

Not hearing any response, the man reached into his jacket and pulled out a Smith & Wesson Model 500 Revolver and aimed it at Lucy.

'Where is he?'

There was no time to respond, fortunately, as Lucy was ready to give up the trembling man. It would have been foolish for her to risk her life for a stranger.

Sirens went off in the distance.

The guilty man grimaced and then used his pocket square to wipe off the gun and drop it onto the floor. Without a word, he then turned around and ran, clearly not wanting to risk running into the police.

Hilda quickly picked up the revolver from the floor. It would have raised unnecessary suspicion if a policeman or basically anyone would have seen it lying there. In a worrying gesture of blind faith, she walked around the counter and handed the gun to the trembling man.

He took the gun from her with both hands. He placed the weapon in his suit and then looked up at Lucy who stared at him with intense concentration. The trembling man stopped trembling and looked at Lucy with a mixture of gratitude and relief. Finally catching his breath, he threw one last glance at the door and stood up.

Extending his hands, he said, 'Hi, I'm Harvey.' His words were polite, formal and charming.

'I'm Lucy.'

She shook his hands.

The touch sparked something within Lucy, possibly the alien feeling of warm love, but there was no indication of a mirrored feeling.

'So what was that all about?' asked Lucy finally,.

Harvey chuckled and answered, 'Just some Christmas fun.'

three

THE LONDON POLICE headquarters, more popularly known as the Scotland Yard, was a dense building full of urgency. Constables, both uniformed and plain clothed, were centred on this very establishment waging their endless fight against crime.

In the force's special office—based out of an apartment in a secondary building—designed for special investigations, two men sat on the eighth floor in a converted two bedroom flat overlooking similar buildings surrounding it.

The tiny flat, which held a little plaque on its entry door titled 'Diplomatic Affairs' was a brooding yellow which starkly contrasted with the two gargantuan wooden desks that rested on either end. Light from the sun palely coursed in through the windows, blending in with the organized mess of paperwork laid across every surface imaginable.

Two men, in black suits, were sitting behind the desks on either end, looking into each other's eyes, communicating wordlessly as people often can after spending years together.

The man on the right end was Chief Superintendent Lomax and the man on the left was Chief Superintendent Hult. Lomax and Hult had been a team ever since they joined the academy together. They were even promoted together, cracking down big cases as partners.

Now, handling the Diplomatic Affairs division, they put their talent into special and covert cases that would've been too delicate for other members of the force. For this they were compensated separately and generously.

'How was Christmas, Lomax?' asked Hult.

Lomax checked his watch. It read '26/12'.

He chuckled and replied, 'Huh, I guess it was Christmas yesterday. I thought it was just the weekend.'

'Not much of a celebration with the parents then?' Hult continued.

'They're off on a cruise somewhere,' answered Lomax, 'What'd you get up to?'

'Went to meet wife's parents.'

'How'd that go?'

'Well, they got me a Tag Heuer watch, which was quite nice. The gulf kind I think, the kind of watch I'd wear with a tux.'

'Fancy. Anything eventful happen?'

'Well, my father-in-law had a heart attack during dinner. Passed away, sitting at the table. It was a shame, everyone started sobbing so I couldn't even finish dinner. Did I mention they had just the best pudding for desert? I was half way through the pudding when he popped. It felt rude to even take a bite after that. Though, I seriously considered it.'

'There must have been a lot of crying then. I really hate it when people cry.'

'Yeah, it was horrible. Just tears everywhere. I got out of there as soon as I could.'

'When's the funeral?'

'Tomorrow. It's going to be all stark and depressing. I mean, funerals should be happier. More like a farewell party as someone says their goodbyes and takes a trip up to paradise heaven.'

'Hopefully, it won't last too long then.'

'Well, I'm trying to convince my wife and her mother to make it an open bar event; might make things more cheerful and bearable.'

'I'd like that. If you manage to swing an open bar, send me an invite.'

'There's already one in your mail.'

There was a knock on the door.

A small man entered. He was also wearing a black suit. Hult and Lomax looked at their small comrade with disdain as he almost always bore bad news.

'What's the update, Ratman?' Lomax asked.

Chief Superintendent Rudolph Ratman had been cursed with a surname that would be the cause of many troubles in his lifetime.

'There's been a report, and I think it's your guy.' Ratman shared carefully.

'What's the situation?' enquired Hult.

'We have a report from the Edinburgh Police,' began Ratman, 'that an Arabic man shot a bystander in the neck while chasing a man named Harvey Hyde through the high street. The perpetrator was dressed in a luxurious suit and had an unusually handsome face, as described by eye-witnesses. After a short chase, both men disappeared into an alley.'

'Looks like our man's still after Hyde,' said Hult.

'I'll book our flights to Scotland,' confirmed Lomax.

four

It was another slow day for the shop. Lucy stood around waiting for customers to roll in while Hilda prepared some fish for the evening rush. Lucy still dwelled on the events of Christmas. She was enamoured with Harvey Hyde. Not only he looked handsome, but the fact that she had seen him at his most vulnerable, had drawn her to him.

'Stop thinking about him, Lucy. He's no good for you,' beckoned Hilda from the back

'I'm not,' lied Lucy, as she stared at his name and number on her phone.

'Call me if he comes back,' was the last thing Harvey Hyde had said to her that day. He had worried that the man hunting him might return to Lucy's shop. Lucy didn't care, as long as she had a way to reach the man she had fallen for, she would eventually find any excuse to contact him.

The door swung open and two men in black suits walked in. They both had pristine side-parted black hair and looked like hateful twins. Golden police badges glimmered from their belts and suddenly Lucy was on guard. Harvey had told her quite clearly to say nothing to the police.

Lomax and Hult were not impressed by Lucy's Fish &

Chips shop. They stood around observing their environment, both secretly hoping for a CCTV camera that would simplify their lives beyond comparison. They were not that fortunate.

'So, who owns this successful establishment?' asked Lomax.

'Me,' answered Lucy with hesitation. As strong as she wanted to be, the police were intimidating, especially Lomax and Hult.

'And what's your name, sweetheart?' asked Hult.

Hilda turned extra cautious in the kitchen. She didn't like the vibe these two men gave off.

'Lucy,' she answered.

Hult chuckled and turned to Lomax.

'Chief Superintendent Lomax, apparently this place is owned by this young lady over here and her name is Lucy,' Hult spoke with intimidation, playing with Lucy's strength.

'Chief Superintendent Hult, are you saying that Lucy owns Lucy's Fish and Chips shop? I never would have guessed.' Lomax replied to Hult while baring an evil grin towards young Lucy.

Lucy was intimidated and rightfully so. But she remembered her feelings for Hyde; she could never honourably betray those.

'What can I help you with, Sir?' asked Lucy, regaining her confidence.

Hult smiled and answered, 'We're looking for two men. An Englishman named Harvey Hyde and a man from Dubai named Hussein Malik.'

'Why are you looking for them, sir?' asked Lucy.

Hult turned to Lomax questioningly. Lomax nodded in return. They needed to confirm with each other that they were agreeing to share information with Lucy.

'Well, Lucy,' began Hult, 'I'm not the wordsmith that my partner Lomax is, but I'll do my best to describe the situation to you. You see, recently Hyde returned from the UAE having spent a month there. We do not know what he did there and whom he angered, because upon his return he has been followed by Hussein Malik who seems to crave the death of Hyde. Just a few days ago, Malik shot dead a hotel security officer who attempted to restrain him as he hunted Hyde, and again on Christmas he shot down an innocent bystander. So I hope you understand why we are curious to find them.'

'Are you going to arrest Malik and put him on trial in the UK?' Asked Lucy, relying on what little knowledge she had on International Law.

Lomax joined in, 'Not at all. We're going to arrest and ship him back to his golden palace in the desert. You see, Hussein Malik is the oldest son of the Malik family of Dubai. The family is powerful and wealthy beyond our comprehension so we wouldn't want to do something as silly as angering the entire UAE government.'

Lucy stood quietly thinking.

The two Chief Superintendents gave her a few minutes.

After a while, Hult asked, 'So, have you seen these two men?'

Lucy made her decision and simply shook her head.

Lomax scoffed. Hult flashed a look of disappointment.

five

A GLEAMING TOWER OF modern design, the Blackwood Hotel stood gallantly high on the fringe of the city. Having only been opened a month or so ago, it still smelled like a brand new hotel and Harvey Hyde considered himself lucky to be enjoying its top-class facilities. He stood in the library of the business centre on the eighth floor looking down through the massive one-way window. His polished black shoes stood out against the white fur carpet accompanying the traditional wooden walls. Black seemed to be the furniture's theme: black luxury couches, modern black coffee tables lined with expensive leather.

Harvey was calling Winterfield for the second time this morning and again he received no answer. It was a small matter that needed to be clarified, but it was something that was better taken care of right away.

He put the phone in his pocket, deciding not to call again.

A waitress behind him brought the coffee and doughnut he had requested and placed them on the table. After she left, he took his seat and enjoyed his breakfast. A few minutes later his phone vibrated.

It was a text from Winterfield. 'What is it?'

Hyde found the message a little odd—short and rude. Usually, Winterfield worked to maintain a good relationship with him.

Harvey replied quickly, 'Glasgow Project; how much do we own?'

Two minutes passed before Winterfield finally answered his question, 'We own 60 per cent, JVP owns 40 per cent.'

Harvey thought about his boss's usage of the abbreviation, JVP, instead of actually referring to the name of the company. A Joint Venture Partner (JVP) could have been anyone and it showed the disconnect that existed between the project and the Chairman of the Board. He made a mental note of the matter. Either way, owning the majority had been a good sign. The decision making power was always instrumental in disputes and negotiations.

Two large men in suits stood guarding the door to the library of the business centre. It was a quiet, secure place for important meetings and Harvey had spent almost a thousand quid in bribes to ensure that it was his private space whenever he needed to have a meeting in Glasgow. It had been worth it, each of the eleven times he had used the space.

Today would be the twelfth.

A man named Arnold Ray entered the room ten minutes late for the meeting. He was never happy when someone failed to be punctual.

'I'm sorry, Mr Hyde, I got late dropping off the girls to school.' Arnold Ray offered a pathetic excuse.

Both men sat across each other with the remains of Harvey's coffee and doughnut between them.

'Our project, is it important to you, Arnie?'

'Of course, Mr Hyde. It's the most important project for Lateral Engineering. We are so delighted to be working together with Winterfield Estates on a JV. But, please don't call me Arnie.'

'If you are so grateful, Arnie, you might want to make more of an effort in getting your kids to school on time. You might have time to spare, I don't.'

'I do apologize, Mr Hyde, but please don't call me Arnie.'

Harvey ignored him and pressed a buzzer on the little radio the business centre had provided him. A few seconds later, the waitress entered and asked Hyde, 'What can I get you, Sir?'

'Bring a bottle of Bollinger for me and Arnie here,' Hyde requested

The waitress nodded and moments later returned with the champagne and two glasses.

Harvey grabbed the bottle and popped it open with expert precision. He then poured himself a glass, not even offering to fill that of the man across him.

'Champagne at this time of the day, Mr Hyde?'

'Are you judging me, Arnie?' retorted Harvey.

'Not at all. I was just wondering what is the cause for celebration?'

Harvey took a sip and then smiled, genuinely satisfied, 'A great man once taught me that it was silly to wait for an occasion to do that which you enjoy. Bollinger is for every new day, Dom is for every new celebration.'

six

THE DRAGON'S BREATH Kitchen was a Japanese food house, the epitome of business restaurants in all of Scotland. Every aspect of it breathed elegance and it had the premium prices to match. One would only be allowed in if they arrived in a luxury car wearing a formal suit, preferably dark coloured, and seemed posh enough to enter the restaurant's doors, shaped in the form of a dragon's mouth. It was located in the back of the Ridge Garden Hotel; its main entrance being straight from the street and a secondary entrance through the hotel itself.

The restaurant was usually quiet, given the matters being discussed within its walls were the sort that were better whispered. The ceiling was painted with bright red depictions of dragons conquering armies of humans and the floors were a dense black marble. The waiters were all Japanese, adding to the authenticity, and the chefs cooked to a standard that impressed even those who disliked the cuisine.

The Ridge Garden Hotel had benefited a lot from the restaurant deciding to locate itself within its premises. Several hotels had made tempting offers to the owner of the Dragon Breath Kitchen but he had chosen the Ridge Garden Hotel for no other reason other than the fact that the Ridge Garden

Hotel allowed the restaurant to have its entrance on the Rising Sun Road. The owner of the Dragon Breath Kitchen clearly knew all the small things that made the big difference; the road, according to him, had been a key subconscious player.

A few had argued that the Ridge Garden Hotel's constrained space had limited the success of Dragon Breath Kitchen. They were wrong. The smaller the place, the more exclusive it becomes.

Having just finished what had been the second most fantastic meal of his life, Hyde exited the Dragon Breath Kitchen with an escort on his arm. He wondered if she realized just how good that meal really was in comparison with other Japanese Restaurants. Her experience with the cuisine was clearly limited; Hyde had noticed her struggle with chopsticks.

Hyde and his lady walked through the lobby. He kissed her on the cheek but his night was cut short when he heard a familiar cackle behind him. He quickly turned around, moving away from the escort as he spotted Hussein Malik in the crowd, aiming his giant Smith & Wesson Model 500 at him.

Hyde cursed under his breath as his face was overcome with fear and desperation. He ran towards the door and heard a gunshot that felt like an explosion. He looked behind and saw a hotel security officer fall to the ground

Two other security guards headed towards him, guns in hand. He turned around and exited the hotel to escape the scene. Hyde dropped to his knees right near the exit with relief. He had survived. A victim had been claimed but it wasn't him.

seven

$\mathscr{I}$N NORTHERN SCOTLAND, Duffus was a tiny village on the fringe of a great institute. It was a small community where every outsider was instantly recognized and gossiped about. Threats were few in such a safe environment, so there was no hostility towards a new face, only a lack of recognition.

It was a cold day. The sky loomed gloomily. The rain behaved mysteriously with the occasional blessing of a shower. The grass stood firm, and one would assume this to be just another day in good old Scotland.

It is strange how tension grips people differently. The ignorant and unaware are blissfully relaxed while those with the burden of knowledge often suffer morosely. The tension today was as unevenly distributed and threatening as one could expect. Something was brewing but its nature was haphazardly unclear.

In a black car up the main road, sat Chief Superintendent Lomax and Chief Superintendent Hult, each munching on a bag of crisps. The car reeked of barbecue and sour cream.

The two policemen keenly watched Hyde. He was standing about fifty meters away in the park on the edge of the road smoking a cigarette, having just stepped out of the local guesthouse. It had been a big relief for Lomax and Hult. They were watching the house for almost an hour and had no idea whether or not he was actually staying there. A report from the local police department had informed them that Hyde had been spotted way up here, but they needed to make sure themselves.

'Do you think he's carrying a gun?' asked Lomax.

'Before I answer that, tell me if you know the brand of cigarette he's smoking. It's lime green, isn't it? Is it one of those Asian brands like Panda or something?' Hult retorted.

'Nah, it's a Sobranie Cocktail Cigarette. Usually a girl's brand but I'm not one to judge. I used to smoke anything I could get my hands on when I was an addict, even the occasional Vogue.'

'That's desperation.'

Lomax smirked. He then asked again, 'So, do you think he's carrying a gun?'

'Yeah, he is. Can't you see it?'

'Where?' Lomax was confused.

'You can see the bulge of a massive Smith & Wesson 500 through his jacket.'

'Isn't that the gun Hussein Malik was reportedly using?'

'Hyde must've acquired it in a tussle.'

The conversation was cut short. A red Maserati GranCabrio that they woefully recognized sped past them and pulled up right in front of Hyde. Hussein Malik got out and aimed a newly acquired Micro UZI at his prey.

This time however, Hyde was a little more confident and he quickly retrieved his revolver. A stand-off occurred.

'Should we do something?' asked Lomax.

'Why?' countered Hult.

'You're right.'

'I hope Malik goes down. I am in no mood to deal with extradition paperwork,' Hult said coldly.

Hyde stood pointing his revolver at Malik, whose gun, however, was a bit more intimidating. For the first time since their fateful meeting in Dubai, the two men spoke.

'You were a pain to track down Hyde.' Malik said, his hair blowing over his perfectly handsome face.

'Are you really going to kill me over one thing I said?'

'Only if you don't apologize, Hyde.'

'All you want is an apology? You've been hunting me down for an apology?' Hyde couldn't believe his adversary.

Malik smiled his perfect smiled and answered, 'That's all I ever wanted, an apology. Give me that and we will never see each other again. However, I cannot let someone go if they disrespect that which is most precious to me and not apologize.'

Hyde smiled, 'Well then, Malik, I'm sorry for disrespecting you and your sister.'

Malik lowered his gun, 'Thank you, Hyde. That's all I wanted. I guess it's time for me to return home.'

Malik turned and started to return to his red Maserati GranCabrio. A loud bang woke up the neighbourhood, Harvey's hand cramped up under the recoil and a bullet ripped open Malik's skull and sent his body falling to the floor.

Malik's words had been honest, but Harvey Hyde was not a trusting man.

In the distance, the black car made a turn and drove away from the scene.

Chief Superintendent Lomax and Chief Superintendent Hult could not help but smile. For them, the situation had resolved itself perfectly. The local coppers could handle it now.

eight

A YEAR HAD PASSED but some wounds take longer to heal.

The princess of Dubai sat patiently waiting for her drink to arrive. She thought about the times they had spent together and how he had supported her. It seemed unfair that he was taken away. After all, he had been nothing but good to everyone. Or was it just her that saw such a side of him? She had heard stories of Hussein being a monster but had always waived it off as false gossip or tall tales planted by their few enemies. She couldn't be sure if she would be happy or disappointed by the whole truth. It would be foolish to tarnish the memory of her brother, something still so purely stored away in her heart. But on the other hand she couldn't help but feel that knowing the full truth might help her deal with this loss. Besides, she seemed to feel a growing attachment to her family at this difficult period of mourning together. Hussein could have had a great future, both of them could've had a great future. Vengeance for his murder was necessary. She had considered discussing it with her father but she assumed that he was looking into it already. Furthermore, it seemed unlikely that he would want to contemplate this matter with the most innocent member of the family.

A servant of the house walked in with her drink. It was a strong whiskey. Most had been surprised that the young lady had chosen this over something more soothing such as wine.

'There is some news,' murmured the servant politely.

The princess simply looked at him expectantly.

He handed her a foreign newspaper and pointed to a particular article on the eighth page. It detailed the suicide-homicide of Harvey Hyde and Hugh Rudy by Detective Jin Hanzo. The princess felt mixed feelings. She was happy that the killer of her brother was now gone, but she felt upset that she couldn't thank Jin Hanzo in person for doing her such a great justice.

The Sacrifice of Jin Hanzo

one

DETECTIVE HANZO GAZED at his newly assigned massacre. Jin Hanzo was a veteran investigator for Scotland Yard. His Japanese heritage and brooding aura often alienated him from the rest of the city.

He was a short man with a long face. His hair was cut army short and he had a knack for getting himself into unappealing situations through his condescending remarks. A prime example of this occurred when a local constable on the scene approached him outside the mansion and asked, 'Sir, for how many days will you need us to guard the crime scene?'

It was a question asked frequently by constables to detectives; admittedly, protecting a crime scene was a very boring assignment and he would usually much rather be out on the beat.

Instead of just simply giving him a time frame, Detective Hanzo answered, 'Get out of my face, you stupid bastard.'

Constable Thomas was not expecting such a rude remark. Maybe that's why his colleagues had chosen to avoid conversation with the detective and suggested that he do the same.

Hanzo walked into the mansion. He didn't care about

anyone else's feelings. A lifetime of frustration had driven Jin Hanzo to point of bitterness from which there was no return. He demanded respect for his talents, asked nothing else of the world and expected the world to ask nothing else of him.

Constable Thomas returned to the outer boundary the force had set up earlier. He saw two of his fellow constables, Berry and Crowe, standing around smoking cigarettes in hope that time would magically speed up and the work done without putting in any effort.

Berry and Crowe were both Welsh. Like most people however, living in the dreamscape of London seemed like a welcoming idea, and the thrills of being an enforcer of Scotland Yard pushed them further down the path of becoming patrolling flatfoots. Berry was the taller one but Crowe was wider. It would be difficult to guess which one would win a fight. Berry's height was equally matched with Crowe's muscularity. One would doubt the chances of the conflict being a physical one anyway, guns being much more efficient at getting the job done.

They turned to Thomas as he approached and since they had a few years more experience than Thomas, they knew what his expression meant. Every constable was at least once insulted by a senior officer. Thomas had just completed a rite of passage.

'So what did the Detective say? When can we go home?' asked Berry.

Thomas ignored the question and asked one in return, 'Am I stupid?'

Berry and Crowe chuckled.

'Not at all,' answered Crowe. 'Hanzo just likes to dominate

people by getting under their skin. I bet he has some sort of inferiority complex.'

'I disagree,' countered Berry, 'I just feel he and all the other senior officers like to toughen the constables up. I mean, they're the ones who deal with the really dark stuff.'

'Well, whatever his reasoning, I'm not going to try and understand why he was being rude. I thought the senior officials were supposed to mentor the constables. We're the future of the fight against crime after all,' Thomas announced, optimistically.

'If you really want to fight crime, join Internal Affairs,' said Berry. 'They're the ones who hunt the worst of them; the ones that play both sides of the law against each other for their own benefit.'

Crowe scoffed, 'The Harrison Case?'

'Yeah, the Harrison Case,' Berry defended.

'You really need to let that go,' said Crowe.

'Only when they recognize its importance and put in textbooks,' Berry stated.

'What on earth is the Harrison Case?' Thomas asked.

Crowe moaned. He had heard the story too many times.

Berry cleared his throat and answered Thomas, 'It's the famous tale of Assistant Commissioner Harrison. Four years ago, he was arrested for investigating murders that he himself had committed. You see, aside from being quite a senior member of the police force, Harrison had also played the role of assassin in settling a power dispute within the London Mob. The worst part, when questioned about it, he said that he done it for his great city; by taking a few lives he had saved many. What was that line he had quoted from Star Trek series, Crowe?'

Crowe thought for a second and answered, 'The needs of the many outweigh the needs of the few.'

Thomas considered the tale he had just been told. It definitely sounded a bit fantastic.

'Why have I never heard of this?' He asked his two comrades.

'They kept it very hush-hush. It was an embarrassment for Scotland Yard,' Crowe explained.

'Well how'd you hear about it then?' asked Thomas.

'We have our sources,' Berry tried playing the superiority card. Maybe he was the one with the inferiority complex.

Crowe flashed Berry a dirty look and then answered Thomas, 'Chief Superintendent Lomax got quite drunk at one of our charity events and spilled the story to Berry here. We were asked to keep it to ourselves but since the story's quite old and you look just about a little trustworthy, sharing it with you might not have been the worst idea.'

Meanwhile, Hanzo stood at the door of the mansion, his brain clamouring against a wall created by a severe lack of clues. He studied the doorknob, the door hinges, the door texture and even the sound of the door opening or closing. It was impossible to determine whether there had been forced entry.

Looking for an inexperienced opinion to counter his current theory, Hanzo hailed the Chief Constable standing only a few feet behind him. Chief Constable Woodrow was a cliché of an officer, an average tubby man with a balding head and a foolish face. How he garnered respect seemed to be beyond Hanzo's understanding, but at least the man must have had some talent to get him bumped up at least a rank. Or was it just seniority? Hanzo questioned the benefits of the tradition that existed within London's police force.

'What do you think Woodrow?' asked Hanzo.

Woodrow, who clearly had a theory prepared, offered a response swiftly, 'Well, there are no signs of forced entry, it's definite that the killer was someone the family knew.'

'Wasn't the family murder quite brutal yet mechanical? It does not seem to be a passion killing or personal vendetta. Am I right?' Hanzo checked.

'Well, yes, but what does that have to do with the entry?' Woodrow wondered.

'You see, it is quite unlikely that someone the family knew well enough to let into their home was sociopathic enough to execute them with their bare hands. I think it was someone knocked on the door and when the wife opened to have a chat, he barged in,' Hanzo's explained.

Woodrow nodded in agreement. He didn't see it as his failure that he had not been able to deduce the occurrence accurately, instead he believed that it didn't matter

Hanzo walked into the home. The murder had happened in the lobby that opened up to the left into an open kitchen which further led out into the yard.

The pale red body of Harry Winterfield lay at his feet. The powerful man was now nothing more than a hunk of dead flesh.

The wife lay further away. A part of her cut up leg still knifed into the wall. It was gruesome, but something felt amiss. Several analysts were in the room along with Hanzo, going about their typical business of recording the little things in their note pads and taking photos of anything and everything.

One of them, a man named Carl, approached Hanzo and

asked, 'So, what do you think, Sir?'

The two men had an uneasy friendship after working together a multitude of times over the years. It was difficult to be positive around someone who you only saw when people had been carved up.

'It's prettier than modern art,' joked Hanzo staring into the lifeless eyes of Harry Winterfield.

It was a joke in bad taste but Carl chuckled anyway.

'Something feels amiss, Carl,' said Hanzo, 'What am I missing?'

'There was a boy,' Carl answered.

'Where's the body?' asked Hanzo.

'He's unharmed. The killer didn't even touch him. But he doesn't remember anything. Trauma was too much for him. The psychologists said it would be years before they could safely unlock his memory.'

'What if we unlocked his memory unsafely?' Hanzo only cared about the crime. His mind was focused on the perpetrator.

'That isn't an option, Detective,' Carl spoke coldly before walking away. He may have been familiar with Hanzo but the detective's attitude was difficult for anyone to bear.

two

A FEW DAYS HAD passed and the unstable nature of the case had continued to vibrate.

'You must understand that the boy lost his parents just two days ago. He's traumatized and therefore not speaking at all. He may listen to what you tell him but don't expect a response,' Analyst Carl explained to Harvey Hyde and Hugh Rudy.

'Is he alone inside?' Rudy asked.

'No, he's under the care of Detective Hanzo, the lead investigator for this case,' Carl said coldly.

The conversation was taking place just outside the main gate. It was raining heavily, but that didn't deter Carl from making sure that these two visitors fully understood the situation. He would make them stand there for as long as needed. His respect for the boy's needs was too great to circumvent.

'Didn't any family step in to take care of Sam? I mean, especially with all the wealth behind him,' Hyde said bluntly.

Carl answered, 'They don't seem to have any relations at all. An old aunt but she's in an asylum. Not at all fit to take care of the boy. Detective Hanzo has agreed to look after him for the next six months while Social Services try to sort something appropriate out.'

Hyde and Rudy stood silently.

Realizing that the two visitors understood the message, Carl led them to the house. They followed, drenched in the cold harsh rain. No one seemed to have bothered with an umbrella.

The door opened before Carl could knock.

Hanzo stood in his short black suit staring at the three men across him being pelted by the rain. He didn't immediately let them in.

'Who are these two men, Carl?' Hanzo asked impolitely.

'Harvey Hyde and Hugh Rudy. They were associates of Mr Winterfield and have information to share regarding his death with you and the boy.' Hanzo stepped back making way for Hyde and Rudy to enter. Carl headed back down to the gate for his guard duty.

The three men sat around in the living room. The furniture was fair-coloured and comfortable. The walls were littered with paintings. Sam Winterfield was nowhere to be seen.

'So, what information do you have for me?' Detective Hanzo asked, without wasting any time.

'We would much rather the boy also hear what we have to say. He deserves to know why his family was massacred,' Harvey responded sharply.

Hanzo flashed him a ferocious look, 'Listen to me, pinhead,' he said. 'I don't care what you would rather do. Give me the information or I'll have you both thrown in the slammer for obstruction of justice.'

Hyde didn't flinch. Rudy just watched, alienated. He

assumed the threat didn't apply to him.

Seeing the unrelenting looks in the men's eyes, Hanzo calmed down. It had been difficult few days, even by his standards. The case had become much harder after he had made it his personal mission to look after the boy.

'I'll go get Sam,' Hanzo murmured. Hugh Rudy and Harvey Hyde waited for Hanzo to return with Sam. The two visitors were no longer an Efficiency Auditor and a Structural Engineer, but rather two close associates of Harry Winterfield. In return, they wanted to personally contribute as much as they could in catching the wretched thing that had ended their great boss's life in such a foul manner.

Sam Winterfield was in his sleeping clothes. He drowsily looked at the two men sitting in his living room and didn't even remotely recognize either of them. That instilled grave mistrust and fear within him.

'These men have information about your father's death,' Hanzo whispered.

Sam was now more attentive. He found it odd that everyone always referred to the murder of his parents as his 'father's death'. No one seemed to be concerned with the murder of Linda Winterfield. It seemed that the money and power Harry Winterfield had wielded was managing to buy perks even in the afterlife.

Sam settled onto the couch with Hanzo next to him.

'So, what is it?' Hanzo was now getting impatient. The two men had been a little too restricted.

'Two nights before the murder, I alerted Mr Winterfield to a severe case of embezzlement taking place within the firm. Almost 60 million pounds was being stolen from the company through sub-standard quality development of the SkyStar project. On the night of 17 February, we were investigating the site when we were spotted by the local contractor lurking in the vicinity. He fled before we could catch him. He may have heard our conversation and alerted his co-conspirators. We are guessing that they together or one of them acted individually and decided to take Mr Winterfield out. They're probably coming after us next.'

Hanzo rapidly considered every variable in what he had just heard before asking a question, 'Who all were at the site that night?'

'Just me, Harvey and the boss,' replied Hugh Rudy, breaking his silence.

'And what is the name of the contractor?' Hanzo queried.

'Palmer Tubb. He's a fool though, he couldn't have done this alone,' Harvey retorted thoughtfully.

Sam had heard everything, but not much had sunk in. His brain was fighting any information to do with the incident as he did not yet have the emotional and psychological tools to deal with it.

Realizing that they had done their bit, Hyde and Rudy rose from their seats and tipped their heads before heading for the door. In a rare instance, they heard Hanzo say 'Thank you' as they left.

three

A FEW YEARS PRIOR to Detective Jin Hanzo being assigned the Winterfield case, the man was nothing more than a cocaine-addict policeman accustomed to seeing the treachery in people with disdain in his heart.

In a rather unappealing subsection of Tokyo, there existed a famous establishment named 'The Flower and The Wind'. Brothels never failed to come up with silly names. Despite it being odd to sell an experience so vile and animalistic under so pure and soft a name, the establishment's charm flourished.

Hanzo and Inspector Fujimoto stood on either end of a bronze door. They were both dressed in black suits and in readied breach positions. Each man had a Glock 17 in hand. Inspector Fujimoto too was short like Hanzo, but chubbier. His rounded face made it difficult for him to be intimidating, which was a serious shortcoming in the law-enforcement business.

Hanzo had returned to his home country through an agreement between both countries. He had partnered up with veteran Inspector Fujimoto in order to hunt down a man named Wei. He had escaped from the UK back to Japan despite being wanted in both countries for multiple counts of murder.

They had tracked Wei for almost a week now and discovered that he was holed up here in this brothel. He was a dangerous man and hunting him had been the most fun Jin Hanzo had had in a while. Fujimoto, on the other hand, had a bit more of a serious approach. Pressure from his Commissioner had meant that his reputation was on the line.

Fujimoto signalled a countdown using his fingers. A few seconds later, the two men burst through the door, pistols pointing towards scurrying women and men setting off panic throughout the establishment.

The Madam of the brothel approached the two cops fearlessly while her girls and clients panicked in the background. The neon pink lighting of the rooms made it difficult to identify people clearly.

'May I see your warrant officer,' requested the Madam.

'Out of the way,' ordered Fujimoto.

The lady did not move.

To Hanzo's shock, his temporary partner fired a shot into the old lady's leg. She dropped to the floor screaming. It had been a move of desperation. The panic in the brothel escalated.

A larger bedroom in the back had a neon sign hung on the door that read 'VIP'.

They both jogged towards the door and burst in.

Wei sat on his knees in the middle of the room, his hands on his head. He seemed to hope that his surrender would guarantee his safety. However, his bloody vest and torn trousers did not inspire sympathy.

Behind him on the bed lay a fully-clothed girl. Her face was battered and bleeding. Fujimoto got onto handcuffing his culprit while Hanzo rapidly approached the girl and turned her over to see her face. She was barely conscious, but he was immediately smitten.

She might've been in the filthiest business, but Jin Hanzo, even past her facial bruises and bleeding, could sense her profound beauty.

'What's your name?' He asked.

'Kimiko,' the girl replied.

'Did he do this to you?' Hanzo questioned, referring to Wei.

Kimiko simply nodded in return.

Hanzo backed away from the girl and readied his pistol.

Fujimoto realized his intentions but didn't seem particularly motivated to stop him.

Hanzo fired a single shot through Wei's head. Kimiko shed a tear of happiness which ran down her bloodied face.

'I guess this is easier than a trial,' pondered Fujimoto. The rest of the brothel seemed to be vacant. Even the wounded Madam was nowhere to be seen.

'Should I arrest her?' asked Fujimoto.

Hanzo glared back at him, 'Don't mention her to anyone. I'm taking her back to London with me. That's the only way she'll be safe.'

Fujimoto just nodded. He didn't really understand the reasoning behind Hanzo's words or actions.

four

*B*ACK TO PRESENT day, Hanzo juggled his thoughts between the investigation and the boy whom he now cared for. The investigator always ate his meals alone. It gave him a chance to reflect on his day. This was quite against Japanese tradition where meals were always to be consumed in the company of friends and family, but Jin Hanzo enjoyed taking advantage of the more lenient culture of the west.

Mary's Diner was a quaint young place. It was not too out of the way and was just a road off the drive between the local precinct and the detective's house. It was a bit Americanized with its long food-bar and large leather booths. This put off the more traditional British patron and worked to Hanzo's favour; he wanted to make sure he didn't bump into anyone he knew while enjoying his role as a contributing member of the anonymous public.

He had enquired and the name of the owner wasn't actually Mary. The Diner had been named such because it seemed more welcoming than Mohammad's Diner, especially since the establishment was serving more traditional American foods.

Hanzo devoured his pizza while checking his emails on his phone. He usually just read the news but there had been an oddly high number of messages to him lately and he wasn't particularly enjoying sorting through it.

His attention from his meal lifted quickly. An uninvited stranger took a seat across him. The man wore a fedora and a long black overcoat.

'How's Sam?' asked the Old Man.

Hanzo put away his phone. His fingers itched for the gun in his belt holster. He decided to be civil and reply politely, 'Sam's fine. Who are you?'

In a rare occasion, as though he was laughing at his own private joke, the Old Man said, 'To you, I'm the devil.'

Those words hung in the air as the Old Man retrieved a thin document from within his overcoat and placed it on the table. Hanzo only had to look at it once to understand the immense gravity of the situation.

'Where did you get that?' He asked.

'Lung cancer isn't the kind of thing you should keep a secret, Detective. You barely have any time left at all,' the Old Man spoke coldly.

Hanzo had worked hard to maintain mobility and put on a tough front but in reality he only had a few weeks to live.

'What does my life have to do with you?' asked Hanzo.

'Nothing yet. But if you were to accept my offer, things would change,' the Old Man smiled.

'What offer?'

'Well, Hanzo, I am the man that killed both Harry and Linda Winterfield. I can tell you this because I know you are a reasonable man and what I have to offer you is much greater than what you will gain by arresting me.'

Hanzo remained silent.

The Old Man continued, 'In a briefcase just outside, I have placed half a million pounds in unmarked cash. My offer to you is this: take the briefcase and in return, please dispatch Hyde and Rudy; the two associates of Mr Winterfield.'

Hanzo considered the proposal and then answered, 'I'm gone in a few weeks. The dead have no use for money.'

The Old Man whispered in return, 'The money isn't for you, Detective. It's to make sure that Kimiko is looked after your time has come.'

five

A MUSEUM OF TRINKETS. That's what the mayor's marketing team had tried to sell it as. Many would doubt London's need for yet another attraction but it was nice for Mayor Heartwood to be able to list an achievement in his time as the leader of this great city.

Located near Marble Arch, the Marble Palace didn't actually have any marble in its structure. The material had been dubbed too expensive by the budgetary committee to be used during the recession. Fortunately however, the rather large building was in the shape of a palace, greatly adding to its charm and grandeur. The construction had taken place on what used to be a park. London's density grew but the city always had Hyde Park to rely on as its saviour.

The Marble Palace housed nothing but oddities, most of them mundane. Visitors had been disappointed and reviews in magazines and other publications had mostly been mediocre. It was praised by people for satisfying the curiosities of specialists and collectors but offering nothing to the general public.

Within the museum, in the section dedicated to Clocks & Watches, Hyde and Rudy stood facing a grand stopwatch exhibit at 9 a.m. It might've been large but that only magnified its simplicity and sped up the process of boredom. The two men stood quietly as tourists walked around and through them. Most of them were just old couples or grandparents taking their grandchildren out on the town.

Hyde had suggested the Marble Palace for the venue of the meeting as he needed to talk to Rudy quite urgently. The venue for the museum was almost exactly halfway for both of them, not to mention that he did have an interest in actually seeing the museum; it had come highly recommended by his mother. But he had been a fool to listen to her. They had never shared any similar tastes.

'I worry for our safety, Harvey,' said Rudy softly.

Harvey had considered the situation for a long time. He had come to the poorly reasoned conclusion that if something was to happen to them, it would've happened already.

'I think we'll be alright,' said Hyde.

About twelve feet away from the Efficiency Auditor and the Structural Engineer, Hanzo pulled the trigger of his SIG Sauer P226. It was quite the efficient pistol.

The first shot rang out quite loudly. There was an instant echo of screaming. Worried patrons of the Marble Palace fled the scene.

The bullet had been aimed at Hyde. Hanzo was quite the marksman and had managed to score a bullet to the brain. Blood had splattered across on Rudy's fantastic suit.

Rudy first stared at the dead Harvey Hyde and then looked up at the shooter to be even more shocked as he saw Hanzo. The Detective pulled the trigger once again, but this time he hadn't been so accurate. Rudy took a bullet to the shoulder. He stumbled back and shouted in pain before falling to the ground unconscious.

Hanzo was certain that Hyde was dead but he couldn't be sure about Rudy. He didn't have time to check. He could hear Museum Security running towards him from behind; pistols, shotguns and batons in hand.

Hanzo had not planned to subject himself the humiliation of being interrogated by his own police department. Instead, he decided on following through with what he had promised himself. He placed his pistol inside his mouth and pulled the trigger for the third time. Mayor Heartwood was about to face a Public Relations nightmare.

six

THE OLD MAN stood in the lobby of a medical establishment. It was 7.40 p.m. There was white everywhere with the occasional streak of blood which hadn't yet been wiped down. The lights were fluorescent and the sounds were of pain and suffering. The hospital was not the calming home for healing as it had been advertised.

The Old Man stood out quite clearly in the crowd. His long black overcoat and black fedora attracting more than a few looks as people passed by. In front of him was the nurse's desk. Behind the desk was a petite blonde nurse by the name of Lisa. He approached the woman and wielded his weapon, two £50 notes, and gently placed them in front of her. She looked up at the mysterious man across her and then quickly pocketed the money.

'What can I help you with, Sir?' She asked

'Two things—the location of the security office and the number of the room in which Rudy rests,' the Old Man spoke with soft intimidation.

There was going to be no flirtatious banter here, realized Lisa. She couldn't help but be mildly disappointed. She had been working hard to score a rich husband. Her work as a nurse was starting to feel like a drag. At least the occasional thrill such as the Old Man had offered kept things fresh.

He had asked about the security room which was no doubt always a worry. She, however, held no sympathies towards her hospital due to her poor treatment of staff. Neither did she take the doctor's oath, so she didn't care if anyone got hurt

'Security room's down on the right. Mr Rudy is in Room 501,' Lisa answered warmly.

The door to the security room swung open a few minutes later and the Old Man crept in like a phantom. The singular officer lay asleep in his chair. An empty cup of coffee rested on his lap as he was surrounded by dozens screens displaying footage from various cameras across the hospital campus.

He knew the basic system well and approached the console. He typed in a few key commands and the footage from the day was deleted and the cameras were turned off. He hadn't even needed to take out the security officer. The sleeping guard's laziness had saved his life.

It was time to address his real objective. He didn't take too long in finding Room 501. Oddly, there were no guards looking after the door. The fools might've been relying on hospital security. This was going to be easier than expected. The door opened and he silently entered.

Hugh Rudy lay silently asleep in front of him. The two men had never seen each other or spoken but he knew exactly who the other man was. He approached the hospitalized engineer and wrapped his bare hands around his neck. Moments later, the Fletcher Private Hospital lost another patient.

seven

It was the first meeting of the day and still relatively early for most of London. The Mayor's office was of the traditional Victorian garb with an endless amount of wooden flooring, walls and dense wooden furniture. It was all perfectly designed to look contrasting while maintaining a dominating sense of grandness and loyalty.

Mayor George Heartwood was an old, chubby and jolly man. This persona seemed to have worked quite to his favour during the elections. His welcoming face had convinced the people that he would genuinely make decisions based on what was best for the city and not what was best for him. How easy it had been to repeatedly fool the masses over the years.

Commissioner Sigmund Reich of the police sat in the mayor's office watching his boss pace relentlessly. The Commissioner shared a similar body-type to the mayor but was dressed in his traditional blue uniform and was comparatively much younger.

'Do you know why I commissioned the Marble Palace?' asked the Mayor.

The Commissioner thought about it and remained silent. He had no concrete answer.

'I commissioned it Sigmund, because I wanted to give London something to attract a more cultured crowd. Our tourism revolves around people wanting to see the Queen and then spend their nights in sleazy pubs and other hedonistic establishments. No one comes here for the art or the culture. That generation is dying out. I wanted to rekindle it.'

The Commissioner maintained his silence.

The mayor continued, 'And how does my beloved city repay me, Sigmund? Does it build a statue in my name? Does it allow me to pass a bill? Does the local diner create a sandwich in my name? No. Not at all. For that would mean that the people are grateful, and if I've learnt one thing in politics it is that people are never grateful.'

'I can see that you're upset, Sir, but in all honestly ever Londoner fully acknowledges your great contributions to our city,' The Commissioner did his best to appease him.

Mayor Heartwood continued his rant, 'I don't care for acknowledgement, Sigmund. I don't even think I'm upset. I'm just tired. I'm tired of doing everything I can to benefit those around me while they just spit back in my face. I could hand out a hundred keys to the city in a year but who gives me a key to the city? Where is my permanent mark on this landscape? In the history books? No one cares for them. The way technology is going, it won't even be a book after a year. I'll have a few pages to myself in a sixth-form history PDF. Does that seem like appropriate remuneration in terms of prestige for how hard I have slogged to bring the city back up on its feet? Give a man a city to run when all is well, Sigmund, and any fool can do it. Give a man a city to lift out of crippling recession and you'll see if he has the cojones to pull it off. What kind of man do I strike you as?'

Commissioner Reich shuffled uncomfortably in his chair and offered an answer, 'The latter, Sir?'

'Damn right, the latter,' Mayor Heartwood barked, 'I've sweated blood and cried sand to make sure that our employment rate increased, that our teachers were of a higher order, that our unions didn't act too bloody grumpy all the time. And to top it all off, I commission a specialty museum for the people and how do they return the debt to me? No Sigmund, how do you return the debt to me? You allow a goddamn suicide-homicide to take place.'

'I sincerely apologize, Sir. I had no idea that Detective would ever act like this.' Commissioner Sigmund Reich was running low on excuses. Not much could be said to defend what had happened.

'You had no idea, Sigmund? Of course you had no bloody idea. But the bigger question is that even if you did have an idea, would you have been able to do anything about it? If by the miracle of God, you had been given a hint, a letter from a stranger, an anonymous tip, a goddamn police report written by you sent back in time from the future, would you have been able to intervene and intercept? Would have been able to punish the guilty and protect the innocent? Well, let me answer that for you Commissioner of Scotland Yard. The answer is no. You would have failed, just like you have failed already.'

'Sir, we can only investigate a crime after it has taken place. Only in the rarest of occasions can they be prevented.' The Commissioner offered a textbook response.

The Mayor would have lit the textbook on fire given the

opportunity. He bellowed back at the policeman, 'Your words are that of a pessimist, Sigmund. I don't like pessimists. They limit our opportunities. They devour our morale. They crush a successful administration from within. I didn't think it would be you, Sigmund. I didn't think you'd me the man to act as the black hole that would warp my very Government into the realms of inefficiency and failure. But why wouldn't you, Sigmund? Aren't these the realms you call home?'

The Mayor stopped and settled into his grand armchair. The Commissioner was speechless. He was not used to being berated like this but he understood the grief of George Heartwood.

'We know who did it and how it happened, Sir. You've seen the footage. What else can Scotland Yard do for you?' Commissioner Reich offered all he could.

'I want to know why, Sigmund. I want to know why Detective Jin Hanzo shot those two men in my precious new Marble Palace. I want to know why a citizen would want to hurt me after all I have sacrificed to support them,' the Mayor answered.

The Commissioner took a deep breath, 'I'm afraid it had nothing to do with you, Sir. You're just collateral damage; just an innocent bystander.'

The Mayor grew red and growled back at the Commissioner, 'Listen to me closely, Sigmund. You better watch what you imply in this room. I could have that badge ripped off your chest at will. You think I'm insignificant to this city that something as great as this could occur without my well-being even being considered? You're a fool, Sigmund. You've lost your edge. If you don't even realize the role I play in this situation then you're better off handing your rank to someone who can see the full picture. There is no smoke and there are no mirrors here. Just you, me and the cold hard facts.'

eight

In the big office on the top floor, Commissioner Sigmund Reich sat facing Assistant Commissioner Gerald Hooter. The office's entire wall was made of clean and clear bulletproof glass, which overlooked the city.

The floor had a plain white carpet and the main desk was black and covered with thinly layered leather. Medals and certificates of achievement hung on the wall. It was clear that Commissioner Sigmund was proud of his achievements and never failed to show them off.

There were two couches and some chairs on the right hand side, more of a living room area probably used for more casual meetings. While Reich and Hooter usually talked while resting on that furniture, the move to the main desk had made it simple for Reich to communicate just how serious this discussion was going to be.

'I want two very competent men investigating this. There is to be no hesitation in taking any step necessary to get to the bottom of this,' Reich ordered.

Assistant Commissioner Hooter was confused. 'Investigate what, Sir? We clearly saw on the tape who did it and how it was done. God bless CCTV.'

Hooter had hoped the Commissioner would chuckle. He didn't. 'The Mayor nearly bit my head off about this in the morning. He thinks it was personal. He thinks that for some reason, someone had gone out of their way to organize a suicide-homicide within the Marble Arch in order to push the museum and the Mayor's reputation towards failure.'

'Are you serious? This has nothing to do with the Mayor,' Hooter offered.

'I know. That's why we need a team of men who can get down to the actual motive behind the crime so that we can put the Mayor's worries to rest.' Commissioner Reich was not comfortable in his unusual situation.

'Sir, with all due respect, Scotland Yard has more important cases to focus its talented investigators on. We even need a fresh detective to work the Winterfield case,' Hooter tried to explain.

The Commissioner grimaced, 'I don't care how thin we're stretched. Finding out Jin Hanzo's motive is the number one priority. I want some capable men handling it.'

Hooter leaned back in his chair and reflected momentarily. He then replied, 'I guess I'll have to bring in Chief Superintendent Lomax and Chief Superintendent Hult in from Diplomatic Affairs. They're quite capable.'

Commissioner Reich nodded in approval, 'Get them working as soon as possible. I want them scraping every inch of the Marble Palace by the end of tonight. I need to show progress to the Mayor.'

nine

Chief Superintendent Lomax and Chief Superintendent Hult stood examining the crime scene with disinterest. Lomax chewed gum while Hult considered smoking a cigarette. They were dressed in their usual black and could not help be frustrated by the case they had been assigned.

The museum was busy with a multitude of analysts going about their duties and an unnecessarily large number of constables guarding the scene. The mayor had decided that even though there had been a murder, the museum would remain open with only the Clocks & Watches section cordoned off for investigation.

Assistant Commissioner Hooter stood behind the two Chief Superintendents and watched them go about their job with boredom. Hooter was a tall, skinny man with the attitude of an angry parent regarding everything he dealt with. No one really liked him but since he was getting the job done quite efficiently, he was still moderately respected. He had often mused to people and colleagues that he hadn't joined Scotland Yard to become popular, he had joined to put criminals behind bars.

Lomax stood above the body of Harvey Hyde and moved

his blazer. Inside, he saw the massive Smith & Wesson Model 500 perfectly holstered. His eyes glistened as he drew out the weapon and showed it to Hult.

'I really don't want to give this in to the evidence department,' joked Lomax. Hooter was now talking to some lowly constable and was out of audible range.

'That is one magnificent beast,' agreed Hult.

Lomax popped open the chamber and saw that a bullet was missing.

'I wonder where he used the gun. CCTV footage shows that he didn't have a chance to reach for it.'

Hult answered, 'He used it to pop off that Arab prince in Scotland, remember?'

'Oh, yeah. That was a good day.'

Hult retorted, 'No, Lomax. That was a fantastic day.'

Lomax called over one of the analysts and gave him the revolver to place in an evidence bag. Before the analyst could walk away, Lomax whispered in his ear, 'If that gun were to ever be sold in a police auction, you make sure I'm the first one to know.'

The analyst looked at the senior officer before simply nodding in agreement and walking away.

Hooter grew impatient and decided to approach the two supposedly talented Chief Superintendents.

'So, what's the progress, boys? Find anything yet?' Hooter asked.

'Well, I think that's the shooter,' Lomax answered, pointing at the fallen body of Detective Hanzo.

Hooter flashed him a hateful look, 'I'm quite sure everyone knows what happened, Chief Superintendent Lomax. We just want to know why.'

'Don't you mean the Mayor wants to know why?'

The Assistant Commissioner did not answer. Instead he was just faced with another question, this time from Hult, 'With all due respect Sir, why have we been chosen to investigate? This has nothing to do with Diplomatic Affairs. Shouldn't Internal Affairs be looking into why some of our best detectives become homicidal?'

Hooter seemed to have an answered prepared, 'You've been selected because you two have looked into Hyde before and may have more insight than a regular investigator. Secondly, Detective Hanzo is technically a Japanese national, so it is an international incident.'

Lomax and Hult grimaced. It seemed as though this really did fall under their jurisdiction. However, they were looking forward to spring, and their willingness to investigate bloody murders were dimming, no matter how pleasant and enjoyable the act of hunting a culprit was.

The Ballad of Amy Burrows

one

BEFORE HIS INNOCENCE succumbed to the greatest of tragedies, Sam lived in a world of hope tainted by reality. Sam Winterfield was dropped off at school in a Mercedes E350 by Victor the chauffeur. He had been at the service of the Winterfield family for almost half a decade and enjoyed working for them; they paid a fair wage and kept out of his private business. On a daily basis, he was responsible for getting young Sam safely to school and back home.

The car often pulled up right to the door, a privilege usually only reserved for the headmaster but no one ever made a fuss about it. Sam would sit in the back until Victor would come around and open the door and then help him with his bag. Occasionally, when Sam asked him to, Victor would even walk him to his classroom. This wasn't a good sign, and Victor had mentioned it to the Winterfields, but they didn't seem to think much of it.

While Thames International School was pretty far from the actual river bank, it was well respected for guaranteeing good results. Sam hadn't passed the entrance exam but Harry Winterfield had decided to pay his way in anyway.

The school was a big grey building with a blue pattern

that made it appear friendly. Students wore black trousers and a white shirt as their uniform, the standard in most international schools across the world.

Amy Burrows was also a student at Thames International School. Her lifestyle was quite different from that of Sam Winterfield's. The school had often proudly proclaimed that over 30 per cent of its revenue was used to sponsor scholarships for gifted young minds. Over performing in the Thames Scholarship Test put Amy Burrows in that category and allowed her a free ride through the school as long as she behaved well and worked hard.

Amy's father, Michael Burrows, had been exceedingly proud of his daughter. His wife had passed away at childbirth, which helped develop a close bond between the father and daughter. Michael Burrows was an average man who earned his wage working as a salesman. They did not struggle financially but they didn't have much either. So, when Michael saw academic potential in his daughter at a young age, he took her to all possible scholarship events in order to give her the opportunity for a better life.

While Amy qualified in many places and was offered a multitude of invitations, her father had always been the most impressed by the Thames International School. But there was something that always upset Amy when her father would pick her up from school every day. She would always watch her father stare wistfully at Sam Winterfield being picked up in a fancy car by a chauffeur. They never spoke on the drive back home. Michael would only think about how much he'd rather drive that Mercedes, even as a chauffeur, than the withering old Ford Bronco he drove right now. Young Amy, on the other hand, would just listen to the radio and silently resent Sam Winterfield for upsetting her father.

One day, during the mid-lesson break, a furious Amy approached Sam with a geometric compass in hand. Sam shuffled backwards in fear. They were in a corridor packed with students. Nobody interfered; they would much rather gossip later than act immediately.

'Put that away!' shouted Sam weakly.

Amy ignored him and continued to wield her sharp weapon. She leaned in closer to him. Her brain told her not to behave so crudely, but she had seen her father upset enough times to act out.

She yelled, 'Give me your car!'

'I can't. It's my father's,' Sam said.

To Sam, that had seemed like a reasonable response. To Amy, it was just an excuse.

The little girl drove the geometric compass into Sam's arm and he screamed in pain. Tears rolled down his eyes and all the students watched in horror. She walked away, a sea of gasps accompanied by loud screams of pain trailing behind her.

two

Harry Winterfield sat on his leather armchair facing the fireplace. He was grim. His daily solitude had been taken away from him. His wife was in a fit and his son had been hurt.

'I want you to destroy that little girl and her father.' Those were the words of his wife after they had both been explained the situation. Linda Winterfield wanted revenge for her boy who had been in hospital the whole day. The wound had been a deep one.

Harry was thinking with a little more self-evaluation than Linda would appreciate. Where had the Winterfields failed as parents to let their ten-year-old son get stabbed by a female classmate? They were meant to be the peaceful gender. 'Leave the war to the men' had been a traditional motto.

Was his son weak? Had they protected him too much? Harry Winterfield wouldn't hesitate to ask himself any of these questions. To be hospitalized by a ten-year-old girl? That was an embarrassment. His son had let him down.

Linda wanted to press juvenile charges. She didn't care if that bright girl went to jail and destroyed her future. Harry tried to explain rationally. It would be their arrogance to deny young Amy her future. She had gotten in on scholarship. Sam hadn't even passed. She could probably offer the world a lot more than their son could and that was a harsh truth that the Winterfields would have to deal with. Harry had done his best to explain such a situation diplomatically, but Linda hadn't heard a word of it. She phoned the police and Amy was expelled. The young girl's chances of going to a good school or university were instantly crushed. Harry had not been happy with the outcome but he needed to focus on his son.

Sam lay in the hospital bed. He was mildly awake and his arm was covered in bandages. Linda kept weeping. Harry stared at the boy with pity. He was a victim of the world and needed to be protected. He was not cut out to be the kind of strong ones that could conquer it.

Harry leaned down towards Sam and whispered lovingly in the boy's ear, 'As long as I'm around son, no one is ever going to hurt you again.'

Unfortunately, one could assume that Harry Winterfield's promise would die with him.

three

THE NEWS OF the suicide and homicides in The Marble Palace had been the biggest news in the morning's paper. Sam Winterfield had read the article repeatedly even after getting news of the situation last night. His trust in new faces had died away. He was going to need to rely on someone he had known for a long time. Unfortunately, there was only one such person left in his life.

In the driveway of the house, the family's Jaguar XJL stood readied and Victor stood waiting alongside it. Harry Winterfield was a luxury car enthusiast and often bought a new car every year. Sam hoped to carry on his father's tradition in the future.

He stepped out his house in the clothes he had slept in and had made no effort to look even remotely presentable. The chauffeur noticed but made no effort to comment on the boy's appearance.

'What can I help you with, Sir?' he asked.

'I'm guessing you heard about the Detective,' Sam murmured.

'I did. It was quite unexpected. I guess people are a lot more unpredictable than I had thought.'

'I lived with the man for two months, Victor, and never did I once think that he would do something like this. It makes no sense.'

'The world is a harsh place, Sir,' Victor said

'I've been thinking about it. When Social Services eventually comes around looking to find a new guardian for me, I want it to be you.'

He had matured really fast ones the two months.

Victor was taken aback and asked, 'Are you sure, Sam?'

He had called the boy by his first name, in a moment of affection for his young master.

Sam nodded.

Victor considered the situation. Accepting the role as guardian made a lot of sense. He would probably give Sam the best care and the ample funds available to the family would mean that he would still be able to live comfortably.

Sam looked up at the man in front of him. Victor extended his arm for a handshake. Sam shook his arm and added, 'You're still going to be my chauffeur though.'

Victor chuckled at the little boy's arrogance 'Sure thing,' he said.

four

SEVERAL YEARS HAD passed, the stabbing had gone from being the talk of high-society to a faded memory that would only be recalled as a warning to future generations. Life has a way of having a cyclical aspect to it and one could not hope but underestimate the value of such a phenomenon and the often bizarrely beautiful situations that it carried with it.

Sam Winterfield stood alone at the main gate. Everyone knew him as the orphan and no one doubted his need to stay distanced from the rest of society. He had never gotten closure for his loss and that would drive anyone to the breaking point. The boy had gotten much taller and much smarter in the past four years. No longer sheltered by his parents, he had come to rely on himself to get everything done and while it had been overwhelming and intimidating at first, he had overcome his obstacles with help from Victor.

As Sam waited to be picked up, Amy walked up to him and without a word locked her hand into his hand. Amends had been made in the past few years and Sam had ensured that her future was once again safe. The school had been made a donation big enough for them to open the Winterfield Library. In return, they had removed the probation from Amy's records and allowed her back into the institution. In addition, Victor had to deliver a big fat bribe from Sam to his contact at the police station to make the incident report disappear. Sam had also given Amy's father a job as an Additional General Manager at Winterfield Estates, and the Mercedes E350 he had craved so badly.

Sam had understood why Amy had acted the way she had. Losing his family himself had made him sympathize with her actions and led him to realize that it hadn't been the right of his mother to take away her dreams.

Amy, in return, had felt nothing but powerful love and gratefulness towards Sam. Her father had been as appreciative. Both of them had matured into young teenagers, and quickly developed feelings for each other. Their emotional bond had been much too strong to ignore and a little family of their own had formed. Christmas and Thanksgivings involved Amy, her father Michael, Sam and Victor gathering at the Winterfield Estate to celebrate each festival.

Within the school, where money was a disadvantage, Amy was Sam's protector. The young Winterfield was broken after being orphaned and often could not control his temper. On one occasion, after being subjected to a rude joke about his parents from an older student, Sam had stabbed him in the rib with a scissor. The older boy had been hospitalized for two whole days, but, of course, the school decided not to interfere. In addition, upon Michael's recommendation, Sam had sent a briefcase with £50,000 to the home of the student to settle the matter with his parents and make sure that he changed schools. Since then Amy had taken it upon herself to ensure Sam never faced such a situation again. It always ended up hurting them the most.

Sam and Amy stood quietly, holding hands. They knew each other too intimately to constantly have to share words. Teachers walked past them and so did the occasional glaring student. They were the only couple in the school that didn't get told off for public displays of affection. Well, Sam was an exception to most rules. He was like a little adult who had negotiated a role within the school society. A meeting between Victor and the Headmaster had made sure that there were clear guidelines about how Sam and Amy were to be treated. Sam didn't do homework, he skipped as many days as he liked, and was often rude to teachers but no one was allowed to say anything to him. Even the other students loosely understood the reason. Amy, on the other hand, was still the model student. She would occasionally get teased about the stabbing incident, but a few words from Sam would resolve the matter quickly. Sam had also made sure that Amy became Class President and then School President. This had been non-negotiable when the donation for the library was being discussed. The Headmaster of the school had agreed to such requests, the sum of money being unusually large.

Sam and Amy's wait ended as the white Rolls Royce Phantom pulled up. Both of them got in the back seat, and though Victor was expected to be present, they were surprised to see Michael sitting in the front passenger seat. Everyone in this little dysfunctional family addressed each other by their first name (except Amy, who called Michael 'Dad').

'We thought we'd surprise you,' said Victor, as he sped away from the school.

Michael looked back and smiled. Amy leaned forward

and gave him a hug.

'Where are we going for lunch?' asked Sam, flatly.

'We thought we'd head to Lakeside Hall?' Michael offered with a smile. He was dressed in a beige Armani suit. The traditional wear of Winterfield Estates employees.

'Again?' asked Sam.

Amy flashed him a look of concern, 'But Sam, Lakeside Hall is your favourite restaurant.'

Sam let out a deep breath, 'I don't feel like it today. What's your favourite restaurant?'

'Would Peach Garden be okay?' Amy asked.

Sam smiled, the way he only would at her, and answered, 'Anywhere you want.'

Victor had heard the whole conversation and couldn't help but smile at their love. He changed direction.

five

THE PEACH GARDEN restaurant offered a dynamic decor. The walls were spaced and well-gapped to allow the patrons to enjoy the wonderful British weather. The walls alternated between a yellow and maroon colour, while the ceiling was pure glass with white boundaries, divided into several medium-sized misaligned squares. The floor was wooden with a cheap pattern, surprisingly out of character for such a nice restaurant.

Amy, Sam, Michael and Victor stood at the entrance waiting to be seated.

Michael, standing ahead in the group, was approached by the hostess who had a disappointed look on her face.

'I'm sorry, Sir,' said the hostess gloomily, 'but we don't seem to have a table, at least not for another hour.'

Michael pointed to a vacant table in the back, 'What about that one?'

The hostess looked at the table. She tried to explain with hesitation, 'Well Sir, that one's reserved for a special guest.'

Michael reached into his pocket. He retrieved four £50 notes and placed them in the hostess's front jean pocket. 'We're those special guests,' he said.

The hostess smiled. She wasn't going to let £200 be worth

less than an apology to her boss. 'Sure,' she replied, before leading them to the table in the back.

They settled into their usual positions, with Michael and Sam across each other, and Amy and Victor across each other. Mostly, Victor and Michael talked business while Sam and Amy had their own cosy chat. Unlike most fathers, Michael trusted Sam with his daughter. He knew Sam loved his daughter, and he genuinely relied on her. He had also probably done more for Amy than her father ever could.

Amy turned to Michael to discuss her day at school. It was exciting that he had surprised them by joining them for lunch.

Sam and Victor were discussing a more serious topic, something that had been weighing on him for quite some time. 'Victor, I've been doing a lot of thinking. I know you've told me to forgive and forget, so have many other people. I understand why you say this but even after four years I can't. Every night when I sleep I dream of their faces and every waking moment my hatred for their murderer grows colder in my heart. I need closure in my life. I want to meet the man. I want to end him. I want to take away from him as he has from me.'

This had been the subject for countless hours of discussion between him and the boy. 'Killing him won't make you feel better,' Victor said.

A quiet moment passed as Sam considered the path that lay ahead of him.

Victor exhaled, looked across at Amy and Michael. He was proud of Sam for trying to start a new family. He was proud that he had managed to forgive and forget. He was proud that the young boy had done so much for two people who were strangers at the time. But at this moment, he realized that young Sam was changing every day. The good inside him was being consumed by anger. The only way to overcome it was with some good old-fashioned vengeance.

six

A LONG TIME AGO, before hope was buried within the sands of time, Victor stood outside the home wiping clean the owner's Maybach 62. It was his first day on the job and he couldn't help feeling a little nervous. The car was the most expensive he had ever driven. And he had heard of the grand stature of his new boss; he was intimidated.

Victor Winkle was born and brought up on the outskirts of Surrey. His parents had been farmers. Most of his childhood, he hadn't seen much of any big city. Tending the cattle and driving the tractor had been his big adventures as a young boy in the 1970s.

School for him had been a boring exercise, a small local one aptly titled, 'Nest Public School' that hadn't done much for his development except ensuring a high-school diploma.

Hard work as a child had ensured that he turned out as a medium-height but well-built man. However, the protected innocence of rural England had put him at a great disadvantage when he first entered London, the grand hub of the UK.

His father had threatened and begged him to not leave their home and farm, but it had been to no avail. Ever since he watched too many films on TV about the big city, Victor had craved the lifestyle of an overpopulated urban jungle.

His father Carter Winkle, the head of the local farmer's market, was a ripe old crank that never failed to squeeze in a World War II story whenever he had the chance to. Having shot countless soldiers as a teenager, the man now craved peace and had retreated to a piece of farmland that had been bequeathed to him by a long-lost uncle. Over time, he had become weary of the cities he had once so fondly fought to protect. This was quite likely; the selective reporting done by newspapers painted the big cities in an unappealing light, voluntary prisons run by the rich.

Worrying for his son, Carter had begged Victor to not go and had even threatened to cut him off. But right after graduating high school, Victor had packed a bag of everything he owned and hopped onto a bus that headed straight for London. He had not a quid in his pocket and not a single friend in the city.

His first evening had been intimidating and horrible but he managed to hold his ground and walked down to a pub known as the Jockey's Delight, near the bus station where he had been dropped. The barkeep was a man named Ricky and an arrangement had been struck immediately. Victor would have a place to stay as long as he did chores around the bar. There was no cash remuneration involved, meaning that most of the time Victor ended up exploring the city without a penny in his pockets.

However, things went out of hand when a local policeman came to know of this arrangement. Not paying minimum wage was illegal and the situation was made to seem worse by the naivety of the young boy. Ricky had been quickly arrested and the Jockey's Delight was closed down leaving Victor once again homeless.

The policeman had pitied the young boy and found him a job at a local corner-shop as a shelf-stacker. The boy didn't have any other options and as long as he was getting paid minimum wage, he would get by. The owner of the corner-shop was doing well running a cock-fighting ring and poker club in the basement. Victor was of course paid an extra ten quid a week to make sure that he was blind and deaf to any illegal activities taking place around him.

The corner-shop owner's son was a boy named Simon Shutter. He was a year younger than Victor, which had led to them becoming good friends. Simon often urged Victor to write to his family but he always shrugged off the idea. He would only write a letter to them once he had made something of himself.

After two years working as a shelf-stacker, the owner of the corner shop promoted Victor to cashier. The very same night, Simon drove up to the shop in a brand new Volkswagen, albeit the cheapest one at the time, and took Victor for a drive. Having promoted Victor and buying his son a new car, it seemed that things were prosperous for the corner-shop.

Simon and Victor cruised around London for a few hours. They were now able to travel quite easily and explore places that they hadn't had the money to before. Being the age they were, they did their best to find the cheapest pub with the prettiest girls. But such a venue did not seem to exist.

On the way back, when the boys were just a mile or two away from home, Simon offered to let Victor drive. The boy had grown up in a rural area and his experience had been only with tractors. He was immensely grateful as he sat in the driver's seat of a car for the first time. He clearly had a talent for the thing and instantly picked up the skill required to drive smoothly. Cruising in a car made Victor feel at home and he instantly knew what he wanted to focus on for the rest of his life.

It started to snow and Victor felt foolish for working so hard on keeping the Maybach 62 clean. Fortunately, the boss did manage to get a glimpse of his work as the door to the mansion swung open and Harry Winterfield stepped out and descended the steps. He eyed the quality of the car and then looked closely at Victor.

'So you're the new driver?' asked Mr Winterfield.

Victor simply nodded politely in return.

The boss continued, 'Linda usually makes good decisions. I hope she didn't break that streak by hiring you.'

The driver replied politely, 'Don't worry, Sir. I'll look after you and your family.'

The Paranoia of Richard Fern

one

PALMER TUBB WAS afraid. Things were getting out of hand. He sat in the chair he now seemed to frequent, staring at the pale Richard Fern across him. They both maintained a silence that was unpleasant and demanding. Trust seemed to have faded away.

'I thought we had agreed,' Tubb said softly.

'We had,' the banker retorted.

'Then why did you tell him?'

'Wait, you think I told the Arab about Rudy and Hyde? I thought it was you. There was no way I was going to let the deaths of two men hang on my conscience.'

'How could I tell him? I don't even know how to contact him,' rebutted Tubb.

Trust grew back as the two men realized that they had a common enemy. The Old Man might've not spoken to either of them at all. Was it possible that he had somehow managed to discover the rest of the story by himself? Such a scenario worried Fern. It suggested that maybe, and quite possibly, the Old Man had now begun to act independently and solely for his own interest. He was no longer a part of the group that had decided to steal from Winterfield Estates together, and that made him a threat.

'Do you think he could come after us next?' Fern asked hesitantly.

Tubb took a moment to think. He was an optimistic man so he decided against it. 'Why would he?'

'He's unpredictable and powerful. A man like that has an unlimited set of options. To him, life simply exists as a pattern of risk and reward to satisfy his own needs. If he considers us obstacles, then it might be a good time for us to start worrying,' Fern suggested.

Tubb leaned back in his chair. He was sweating profusely under his suit. 'He seemed like an honourable man. Don't even the most fearsome psychopaths have some sort of code of honour?'

'Honour is a relative subject, Palmer. What we consider honour may be very different from what he considers it to be. We need to understand that if the time comes, our lives could hang in the balance with that Old Man deciding our fate. He may have been a useful partner in business, but I wouldn't trust him when it came to anything else.'

'Do you think he'd do it for the money?' Tubb wondered.

'Of course, my friend. The world revolves around money. You must be very naïve to not understand that. Given his history, he may enjoy such sadistic pleasures as well but in the long-term we were fools to trust him. Why would he settle for 20 million when he could take both of us out and have the full 60? He's taking the risk by going on a homicidal rampage anyway.'

'I guess you're right. I may hire some private security. You should too.'

'Don't be a fool, Tubb,' countered Fern. 'You spend that kind of money and the cops are bound to come knocking. They'd probably arrest you for Tax Evasion if not larceny and association to murder.'

'I guess you're right.' The contractor was feeling cornered.

'I do feel guilty though,' Fern confessed.

'Why?'

'I was the one who gave the Old Man the dirt on Detective Hanzo. But I had no idea he would use it like this.' Fern let out a sigh of failure and guilt.

Tubb leaned further back in his chair. He didn't know how to react to that information. Their scam had gotten much too complicated and they had put themselves at a lot more risk than they had signed up for. And it was all because of one man and his lack of guilt or morality.

two

RICHARD FERN SAT alone in his office wearing a navy blue suit and a white shirt. He stared at the fern that he had purchased. It was a joke that had overstayed its welcome. His eyes were grave; he clearly hadn't slept well in the last few days. To some, he had now become a decision, an option to stay alive instead of 20 million pounds. He was objective enough that no one would pick him over the money. They would be foolish to. He needed to defend himself. He needed to make sure that he was the one making the decisions regarding life and money.

The landline on his desk buzzed. It was his secretary. He pressed the red button to allow her into his office.

Jacqueline Sanchez had been working for Richard Fern for quite a long time. She had initially come to London in the hopes of become an actress but while she was very beautiful, she didn't have any of the other skills necessary. She stared worriedly at her boss. He had been exhausted lately and always seemed to look worse after meeting with that horrid sweaty contractor. He had even begin to act suspiciously by keeping things from her, which was quite unusual behaviour as she, like every other secretary in the building, had signed a confidentiality agreement while being employed by the Boxler Banking Institution.

In her hand, Jacqueline held a package the size of an A4 sheet. It was wide and heavy. That wouldn't have caught her attention, but it was the fact that her boss had strictly asked her to not open it. She had known that that package was the one her boss had referred to because it had no markings of any sort. It was just wrapped in black paper.

Richard saw his secretary with his package and, without a word, pointed at his desk. She left it on the table and left. Richard stared at the black box with indecision. He had come to a crossroads at his life. If he went through with his plan, he would have abandoned his morality. As a devout Christian he had overlooked some of his sins such as the occasional scam or bribery. But what he was planning then couldn't be forgiven so easily. His decision needed to be quick. If he loses the willingness to act then he would become an obstacle in the path of his enemies. One could only ponder which situation was actually better.

He took a deep breath. He knew that psychologically and emotionally he was as prepared as one could get. He grabbed the box and ripped away the black packaging. Inside was a stainless steel silver container protected by a number lock. Richard had memorized the code. It was his sister's year of birth. The case popped open. It was an AMT Hardballer. It lay on a soft black cushion within the container and the office light reflected off of its polished exterior.

three

RICHARD FERN SAT in his Mercedes ML350 across the street from a little restaurant called The Baker's Delight. He was dressed in a black turtleneck, black trousers and thick black leather gloves. Fighting off the creeping silence within the car, he found himself sinking into a void of crippling paranoia.

On the passenger seat to his left, he had an item that would worry any normal individual. He put on an intimidating gas mask and adjusted it till he could breathe easily and had a good field of vision. He then opened his dashboard and retrieved his brand—new, gorgeous AMT Hardballer and enjoyed the feel of its cold steel in his hand.

The Baker's Delight was a small cosy restaurant that specialized in traditional pizzas. The owner was a pale old man who worked hard to keep people smiling. It was most often frequented by the locals as it had nothing special enough about it to attract visitors from across town. The restaurant had café-esque furniture with small brown tables with matching chairs that were made from a combination of wood and steel. The main counter housed a viewing fridge that displayed different kinds of chocolate cake and there was another bar counter on the opposite end where solo customers enjoyed their meal.

In the middle of the restaurant sat Tubb, enjoying a meat pizza alone. He looked exhausted, eating the greasy pizza with an unusual dispassion.

Across the road from the restaurant, Fern still sat in his car. The gasmask rested comfortably on his face and the gun lay in his grip. He reflected on his life. He had always hoped to be a respectable banker and had been thankful when he had achieved his dream. However, not a man to be easily satisfied, he had opened up different avenues that allowed him to involve himself in dealings of the more legally questionable sort and multiply his riches. But it seemed that the times had finally caught up with him; now he was in a state so desperate that he was planning on taking another man's life just to ensure that there was no future threat to his. Not to mention that an additional 20 million pounds in the bank didn't hurt his motivation. That was the easier part. Taking Palmer Tubb down had to go smoothly if he could even consider going after someone as dangerous as the Old Man.

It was time. The contractor would finish his meal soon and Fern had to act before that happened. He got out of his car and crossed the road. The night was quiet and the road was empty. From a studio apartment on the second floor, a sole woman watched as a man in a gasmask approached the restaurant. Within seconds, she contacted emergency services. The police were on their way.

The road felt cold and distant to Richard. He had become a phantom. The mask gave him a sense of anonymity that allowed him to believe that he could do anything he pleased; it would be impossible to trace it back to him.

The door to The Baker's Delight swung open and everyone stared with fear at the man in the gas mask. He approached Tubb and aimed his gun at the temple of the balding contractor. With a single pull of the trigger, the chubby man's face exploded and blood covered the wall behind him.

As he turned to leave, he realized that maybe murder wasn't as easily forgiven by people as it may be by his god. The last thing Fern heard was the distant ring of police sirens. From behind, a gunshot from a Winchester 1300 Shotgun decimated his torso. He dropped face first on the floor. Over the two dead bodies, the owner of The Baker's Delight stood angrily with his Winchester in hand. He didn't take too kindly to people murdering each other in his establishment.

In another dark corner of London, the Old Man became 40 million pounds wealthier.

The Generosity of Ken Kitano

one

As time passed, organized crime in London evolved along with it. After years of encounters and bloodbaths, two syndicates had emerged as a dominating force in the market. Unlike the way it had been in the old days, where a single family ran a syndicate, the modern organizations had abolished nepotism for its inefficiency and were now sharing the title of their headquarters as the brand for their business.

The Forge was one such establishment located in Vauxhall and the men from The Forge were a force to be reckoned with. Their counterpart was The Kitano Club in Soho. While the name of The Kitano Club might suggest that it many have connections with Yakuza, but such was not the case. Akira Kitano, the owner of The Kitano Club, had been born and brought up in London. His parents were dentists and treated teeth differently than what the Yakuza were reputed for.

The man who ran The Forge was a man by the name of David Darlington. He was a man with a deformed face and often wore a hat to cover up the ugliness. His physical shortcomings had been made clear to him by his family and friends over the years. Now, comments regarding it didn't bother him anymore. To call the man naturally hideous would be incorrect because it had actually been an incident that had disfigured him.

The Forge itself was a fantastic nightclub. Not for the tourists, this club was exclusively for the Londoners who knew what they were getting into. It had often been mentioned in the newspapers, any mob related incident would often refer to 'The Forge Mobsters' which indicated a sincere risk associated with entering the club. London, of course, had no shortage of Cocaine-addicted yuppies wanting in on some life-threatening action or adventure.

The most recent mention of The Forge in the news was an ever popular story on a man that had been arrested for killing two police officers and a thief. A man named James Arlington had come upon two police officers arresting a man that he had thought he recognized. Deciding now would be an appropriate time to utilize his weapon, James had drawn out his Colt 1911 and immediately shot dead the two police officers. Realizing the thief wasn't someone he knew after killing the cops, he then went ahead and killed the thief as well in order to not leave any witnesses. Unfortunately, because this happened on a retail street there was footage of the event from multiple cameras, leaving little room for doubt regarding his involvement in the crime.

James was described to be one of The Forge Mobsters operating in central London and was reputed to have close ties with notorious Mr Darlington.

two

HULT AND LOMAX sat in the Diplomatic Affairs unit. Lomax was a bit more preoccupied than Hult, studying some case files, while the other played games on his phone. The room was quite cold; they both liked it that way. Hult looked at his partner and smiled. He then said cheekily, 'Is that sweat, Lomax? Are you sweating? It's like 16 degrees in this room.'

'You haven't even looked at our new case, have you? This one's going to be fun,' Lomax responded.

Hult was now slightly, and only *slightly*, interested. He asked coolly, 'Fun, huh? That's an interesting by-product of our work. Who're we hunting?'

'A mass murderer,' Lomax replied with a wide grin.

'I love a good mass murderer.'

'Yeah, they're always eccentric, aren't they?' Lomax pondered.

'Well, they're never boring,' Hult agreed.

He then looked into the file that had been assigned to him and Lomax. He felt lucky for being assigned such an exquisite case. His mind had been careful in choosing the word, 'exquisite'. For him a case could be 'good' when there would be a minor challenge to overcome. A 'fun' case offered a big reward for a little work while a 'climatic' case offered big closure after a long period of investigation. However, an 'exquisite' case was rare. Such cases were so unpredictable that no matter how many innocent lives were lost, the raw number of complications always ensured that the two Chief Superintendents thoroughly enjoyed themselves.

This particular case was one that revolved around Kenta Saito. According to the report, Saito's age and place of origin within Japan are unknown but he was reputed to have the build of a tall thin man with abnormally long arms. The first report on him was registered in 1991 when he was arrested by the Tokyo Police for stabbing a butcher in the arm for increasing the prices of his meat. His moves were cold and deep and precise. He escaped police custody and ended up joining the underworld where his identity was protected in exchange for his services as an assassin.

Around 1994, Saito once again resurfaced and become the subject of a manhunt launched by the Tokyo Police. This manhunt was led by Inspector Fujimoto, who failed to apprehend the target. The first reports of Saito in 1994 came in when two teenagers had attempted to rob him but had instead been found shot dead. It was assumed that these two boys were not aware of Saito's nature or reputation. The second incident was when a traffic policeman had pulled over a Toyota Camry but instead of arresting the driver, the traffic policeman was knifed four times in the torso. At the end of 1994, Kenta Saito once again disappeared leaving the police baffled and under severe pressure from politicians.

This was followed by four murders between 2001 and 2006 which were credited as assassinations by Saito for local crime lords. The first murder involved the assassin firing a single bullet from a revolver at the wheel of a speeding motorcycle which led to a fatal crash. The identity of the occupant could not be confirmed due to insufficient evidence but markings on his vehicle that survived the explosion suggested rival gang affiliations. The second incident was the death of casino owner and his wife. Saito had left the gas on in their house and when the victim had lit a cigarette, an explosion wiped out the occupants. The Third hit took place at Tokyo Airport where Saito shot a TV Reporter in a crowd. This was Kenta Saito's most public crime. It had seemed inspired by a rushed time-frame and desperation suggesting future tension between him and the organizations he worked for. The fourth murder was of Lee Feng, a man from the Chinese Triads trying to make headway in Japan. Saito had been quick to dispatch him before he became too much of a threat.

Taking a break from reading the report, Hult looked up at Lomax and said, 'This guy's record belongs in a museum. He must be a legend of some sort in our world.'

Lomax nodded in agreement.

In more recent events as to why this case file had landed in the Diplomatic Affairs unit of Scotland Yard, Saito had flown into London three weeks ago under a false name and passport. He had reportedly been invited here by Akira Kitano, probably as an asset to help with the growing tensions between the two syndicates. In the past three weeks, Saito had become a suspect in two murders. Both murders were of individuals under the employ of The Forge nightclub and were assassinated on separate occasions. The first incident was a car-bomb placed in a Honda Civic that was owned by the victim. The second incident was that of The Forge Mobster being shot in the head from the building across as he had exited The Forge nightclub. Saito had used a sniper rifle which he had left on the scene, while attempting to flee from The Forge Mobsters that had spotted him. He was even caught on tape for a few seconds while escaping, a grave mistake for a so-called master assassin.

Lomax watched as Hult finished. Both were excited to face Saito. He was a real beast.

'How is he hiding?' Lomax wondered.

Hult thought about it and agreed, 'Yeah, I mean a tall Japanese man in London with unusually long arms? He'd stand out like the Statue of Liberty.'

'The Kitano Club must be working hard to protect him. He's probably their greatest asset and biggest liability.' Lomax suggested.

'Are we really getting dragged into a Mob war? I love it when that happens,' Hult spoke, with a hint of sarcasm.

'I bet Darlington is getting furious,' Lomax guessed. 'He's lost two foot soldiers and hasn't been able to retaliate? That must be frustrating. Especially since the rest of the mobsters must be hungry to make Kitano bleed.'

'We need to get into this,' Hult spoke frankly.

'Do we pick a side?' Lomax asked.

'Definitely,' Hult retorted.

'But which one?'

'The one that wins.'

The two quietly pondered the situation. There was a lot that could happen and there was a lot of room for exploitation. But it was always a big step joining in on such matters because right now they were completely out of the limelight, no one would touch them. But if they took one step towards either side, they could find themselves in the heat of war.

three

While their rivals at The Forge operated out of a dingy nightclub, The Kitano Club was reputed to be a classier establishment. It was a nice divide in the market, the rich old degenerates would visit The Kitano Club while their mistreated rowdy children would frequent The Forge. It was even a rite of passage in some families to graduate from one to the other.

The Kitano Club was a burlesque cabaret club that looked straight out of the 1930s era. There was golden lighting everywhere and pale, expensive yellow walls along with roman pillars holding up the ceiling. The occasional horizontal curtain added to the ambience and one couldn't help but notice just how soft the red carpet was.

The main room was distributed into three heights with the back ascending higher. It was the kind of placement one saw in a movie theatre except here the room was littered with little tables for two in the front and larger booths in the back. Most of the patrons were businessmen showing their foreign partners the city or other businessmen out with their mistresses. There was a gentleman's agreement that this establishment did not welcome wives. But nothing ever does seem to be that simple with women. Lately the mistresses themselves had started gossiping, creating a whole new set of problems.

Akira Kitano, the owner of the club, was a charming young man who made it a point to visit and greet every table every night. It gave the establishment a personal touch and everyone could claim that they knew the owner.

On that day, in the office above the main restaurant, Akira Kitano sat dressed in a navy blue suit and red tie facing two men dressed in exquisite black. Lomax and Hult had decided on how they wanted to approach the matter.

It hadn't been too difficult to get a meeting with Kitano. Usually, one would have to pay for the man's time, but such was not the case when the two policemen walked up to the club and flashed their badges.

'So what can I do for you gentlemen?' asked Kitano.

Hult smiled and replied, 'Well, there's a lot you can do for us, Mr Kitano. There's a lot anybody can do for anybody else. It's what you agree to do for us that matters.'

'I guess that's appropriate,' pondered Kitano. 'What did you gentlemen have in mind?'

Lomax took the lead, 'Well, we're big fans of a friend of yours. I mean, I personally wasn't into the old fan club scene but lately Hult has got me convinced. You see, ever since Chief Superintendent Hult was a little boy, he has always wanted to kill people. But to get paid for carrying out the kill? That would be his dream job. To him that's like giving someone money to do nothing but enjoy themselves. You know what they say, "Do what you love and you don't have to work a day in your life." Alas, such was not the case for Hult. He ended up going down the safe route and becoming a boring old copper like he is today. But recently, keeping up with all news to do with assassins as he always does, Hult came across one who seemed to be a dear friend of yours and we thought that we'd be delighted if you would grant us the opportunity to see him.'

The policeman's tone might've been playful, but he had very clearly communicated that he was aware of the presence of the greatest asset that The Kitano Club had ever acquired. To confirm his doubts, he asked gently, 'And who would this friend of mine be?'

'Kenta Saito,' Hult spoke clearly.

Akira Kitano was disappointed in himself. He had let the enemy become aware of his advantage and lost the element of surprise. The upper hand that he had worked hard to acquire in this conflict was diminishing and he would not allow that.

'Why do you want to meet him?'

'To arrest him and charge him with three counts of first degree murder, of course,' Lomax spoke in a light tone. It was clear that he could be incentivized to behave alternatively.

Unfortunately, Kitano's headstrong attitude kicked in and he barked angrily, 'How about I just shoot you both in the head right now? That would seem like a cheap and easy way to solve my problem.'

Hult laughed. Lomax explained why his partner found this funny, 'It seems you underestimate the situation, Mr Kitano. You see, my partner and I, both are carrying Smith & Wesson Model 500 Revolvers. Anyway, if you tried to kill us, you would definitely take a bullet in the face, and I'm sure a few of your henchman would go down as well before my partner and I cease to be a threat. But that would just be the beginning of the problems that The Kitano Club would invite. As you see, Chief Superintendent Hult and I are quite well reputed at Scotland Yard. The Mayor even gave us keys to the city. That just means that if we go missing, the police will tear London apart and when they come upon your little establishment, I assure you that blood on the carpet will be the least of your problems.'

Kitano was beaten. He just wanted to get this over with. 'So what do you want?'

Hult answered coldly, 'I would suggest a nice care package for my partner and I. Ten thousand pounds sounds about right. That's for us making the Kenta Saito case file disappear from Scotland Yard. In addition, I would recommend getting rid of the man yourself. He was probably an expensive investment but I assure you that you've made a bad call, Mr Kitano. He's more of a liability than an asset. We were quite sure it's him after he took out the first two Forge henchmen but after this third one yesterday, we have solid proof to ensure a conviction. You don't need the legal debt. A bullet is much cheaper.'

Akira Kitano let out a deep breath, he hated it when things didn't go his way.

four

AKIRA KITANO AND David Darlington sat side by side in the little waiting room that seems to be the age-old cliché in all medical buildings. They both hung their heads down in shame.

Kitano Dental Associates was a small private practice run by sixty year old couple Ken and Michiko Kitano. The two had been dentists all their lives and were one of the few super-successful niche private practices that competed with the National Health Service. The dentistry was in a small building in Mayfair and usually only catered to rich clientele. They liked to be special and differentiate themselves. These were the same kind of people who went to The Kitano Club at night and whose children would frequent The Forge.

The structure of the compound included a waiting room, within which the two heads of the London organized crime syndicates sat, and two medical practitioners' rooms; one for the wife and one for the husband. Ken had asked his wife Michiko not to come in today.

Akira and David uncomfortably looked at each other and felt even worse when Ken Kitano walked out of his office to the waiting room in a rage. He was an old man but regular gym visits kept him muscular and intimidating. Physically, he could easily dominate either Akira or David.

The old dentist looked at the two crime bosses with disgust, 'You two fools are messing up this city again. Get your asses in my office right now or I'm going to slap you till your faces go red.'

Akira and David rose from their seats and followed the dentist to his office with their heads hanging. Within the little white room, they settled into the small black chairs, while Ken paced around the room fuming with anger.

'You know we're sorry, right?' David offered weakly. His face still covered with a hat.

Akira gave him a look of disgust. They had been through this a dozen times before. A pre-emptive apology was always a mistake.

'Shut the hell up,' barked Ken Kitano. 'You think this is a joke? This is not a bloody joke. You both could wind up dead or worse, in jail. Why the hell do you guys get into these little fights, huh? Real people lose their lives. Three people died this time and I know one more will have to in order to balance the scales. That's four deaths. As a doctor, I think that's despicable. I work hard to keep people healthy while you fools treat life like a game. What would happen if one of your double-digit IQ henchmen decided to get creative and managed to kill the other boss? One of you would die. Then it would no longer be a game. Get out of this business boys, I can't have you fools making me shell out for a funeral.'

'Dad, it won't happen again. I promise,' Akira Kitano tried to sincerely explain to his angry father.

The dentist wouldn't hear any of it. 'You make me so

angry. I often wonder how I could raise two fools like you. How can I be so sensible and you two so reckless?'

There was a pause.

Ken Kitano walked up to David and looked him in the eye. He then whispered, 'Do you want me to regret adopting you?'

Akira was the next to face his father's wrath. 'You make me hope that your mother cheated on me nine months before giving birth to you.'

Akira and David slumped back uncomfortably. To the London underworld, they were fearsome rivals and dangerous mob bosses. To their father, they were stupid brats taking their sibling rivalry a bit too far.

'We're so sorry, Dad,' both David and Akira said in unison, as they had done since they were children.

Ken Kitano looked at them coldly, finally acknowledging their apology.

'So how're you going to resolve this?'

'Well, Akira killed three of my guys so I'll need something in return to keep the balance,' David complained like a child.

Akira hesitated for a moment and then answered, 'I'll put Kenta Saito in the ground. He's the one who took out your guys. Sound fair?'

David nodded. The deal seemed fair to the Dentist as well.

'Now shake hands boys.'

Uncomfortably and forcefully, David and Akira shook hands. It was the worst feeling in the world but it was something they had to do every time they had a fight. Neither of them had the guts to argue with their father. The last time Akira had tried it, old Ken Kitano had smacked him so hard that he'd broken a rib.

One could only imagine the uproar if someone were to discover that the London Mob was controlled by a shrewd old Dentist.

five

$\mathcal{D}$AVID DARLINGTON WAS not an emotional man, but he did remember his old days with a mixture of warmth and wistfulness.

A small ground floor flat served as the residence of the Darlingtons. They were not a wealthy bunch but had enough to get by. It was the kind of house where one had to climb eight or nine big steps to get to the door, traditional British fashion, and the small apartment served adequately for the family.

Upon entering, there was a small living room with a green couch and two luxurious chairs. The floor was wooden and a round coffee table rested on a cheap light-colored rug. There wasn't much natural light except from a window. That too was kept behind curtains. It only showed the view of a largest industrial zone behind the home. There was a kitchen further down, and two bedrooms to the right. Everything was small but the realtor had done well done to describe it as 'cosy'. Gary and Kay Darlington slept in the much larger bedroom while the smaller bedroom next to it was where ten-year old David slept.

Gary Darlington was from Coventry and had moved to

London around his twentieth birthday to pursue a career as a carpenter. He had met Kay on the train down to London and they both soon fell in love and were married. Kay was happy being a housewife and writing the occasional article for local magazines. Gary had struggled to find work as a carpenter, lacking both skills and experience.

Even though Kay had begged him not to, Gary's pride as a man refused to let him see his family go hungry. He borrowed money from a local loan-shark Thompson. The interest had kept mounting up and even after repeated beatings the situation had become clear that Gary would never be able to repay loan. Unfortunately, for the Darlington family, such matters were only resolved in one single unpleasant manner.

On a late afternoon one day, Gary Darlington sat on the dinner table circling adverts for jobs. He needed to get out there and earn something. This was while Kay helped her young son with the day's spelling homework in the living room. It was a quiet day for a usual peaceful family but one that wouldn't end as pleasantly as it had begun.

Gary had been worried for quite some time. He hadn't been dragged to the railroads for a beating in weeks and neither had Thompson come knocking for money. A loan shark never forgave a debt; it was only a matter of time before the goons came knocking.

Two scruffy looking fellows in cheap garb stepped into the Darlington home. Gary leapt up to defend his family while Kay grabbed her son and took him to the back of the room. Little David was used to this kind of situation; it was not the first time these fellows had burst into the Darlington home demanding money from his father.

'Fellows, let's talk about this,' Gary asked, trying to calm the situation.

Both intruders retrieved vials of acid from their coats. Industrial work around town meant these dangerous chemicals were easily and cheaply available. They also didn't raise too much of a concern with the police. It had soon become a weapon of choice for many.

Gary moved back in fear while Kay covered her son's eyes. Their fate was inescapable. The taller of the two goons opened the vial and threw the acid on Gary. The father put his hand up but the chemical burned through his hand then through his face. His screams were excruciating as he fell to the floor. Both Kay and David wept for their loss.

The other goon aimed his vial at the wife and child and hurled his batch of acid at them. Kay did her best to cover her child as the chemical burned through and took away her life. Unfortunately, the weapon was potent enough to scar the little boy's face. As Kay Darlington fell to the floor, the two goons left the premises.

Little David screamed in agony. He couldn't face being in the same room as his deceased parents. Using memory, he navigated out of the apartment clutching the walls and, upon reaching the door, toppled down the stairs onto the road below.

A car pulled up to him and an intimidating Japanese man got out of the vehicle and picked up the little boy. He looked at his face and saw a victim of only the most heinous of crimes. He lay the boy down in the back of the car before rushing to check the apartment. Inside, he found more destruction. He used the phone inside to call the police and then ran back out to his car. The little boy was still wincing in pain and need of immediate medical attention. The man drove as fast as he could to the nearest hospital and was relieved when a few hours later a nurse had informed him that the boy's condition had stabilized.

Two days later, Ken Kitano signed the papers and officially adopted little David.

'He looks like a monster.' Those were the first words that Ken Kitano's wife had said when the man took her, Michiko, and son, Akira, to see the little boy in hospital.

At that moment, Ken had looked at his wife and child coldly and spoken in the gravest tone, 'He is a victim of a monster. Not a monster himself. Michiko, he is your son and Akira, he is your brother. Do not ever question his place in the family. He has been through enough.'

six

It was David's eighteenth birthday. The boy hadn't done well in the past eight years with his severe facial disfigurement. Without his hat and his new family, he might've not even made it this far.

Akira and David sat crouched behind a small wall, watching a large white house in the distance. Akira had worked hard to ensure that he could give his brother a very special gift, the kind of gift that was necessary for the whole family.

Both the boys were dressed in black trousers and black turtlenecks. They would look suspicious if seen from a mile away. But the roads were empty; it was 4 a.m., the night dark as ever. Snow had been scarce but the wind-chills were plenty. Crows croaked in the distance and the full moon served as one of the few sources of illumination.

The night carried a tension that would be noticed by many but felt by few. The clouds in the sky covered the stars and one could not help but notice the thickness of the air. The wind carried the aroma of recently planted shrubs and, a few blocks down, a stray dog had died of hunger.

Akira pulled out two brown bags and handed one to David. They both retrieved the contents and assembled them as they had learnt. It had taken weeks of work but Akira had finally managed to acquire two .38 Snub Nose Revolvers for him and his brother. As the two sons of Ken Kitano stared at the white house up across the street, their blood burned with the need for revenge.

'He lives there alone? Are you sure?' David asked.

'I'm sure,' Akira answered confidently. He had staked out the house the night before.

There was a moment of profound understanding. It was time to act.

The two boys rose and jogged to the house. The cold road silently stood beneath the steps of their expensive sneakers.

The home was a white-coloured duplex. The door was at the end of a small flight of high steps as the lower ground levels were being used as a garage for the owner's car. Quickly peering through the garage window, David saw two cars standing.

David headed back up the stairs as Akira finished picking the lock. The door gently swung open and they entered into a dark living room. They realized that the owner's bedroom must be upstairs. They clutched a neighbouring wall and led themselves towards the staircase and headed upwards. Akira was in the lead and both boys had their revolvers ready for action.

At the top of the stairs, there was a singular door. They composed themselves and then Akira kicked the door down, breaking the immense silence that had hung before. As soon as the boys headed in, David felt for a switch on the wall and finding it, he turned on a light.

The man who had been asleep only seconds before, jumped up and reached for a gun. He was an old man in a silk robe.

There was a Colt 1911 next to him but seeing the barrel of Akira's gun against his face, he decided to not reach for it.

Seeing the two boys who had invaded his home, the man said, 'A Japanese and a disfigured boy? Who the hell are you fools?'

David wanted to answer him but Akira's temper boiled. He pulled the trigger and shot the man in his leg. A loud scream woke up the neighbours. Blood poured out rapidly; the bed sheets quickly went from white to red.

David removed his hat to completely expose his distorted face. Even Akira felt uncomfortable looking at it although he saw it every day.

The man suffered as the boy looked him in the eye and coldly whispered, 'You're Thompson, aren't you?'

The man nodded. He wouldn't lie with two guns pointing at him.

'Eight years ago,' explained David with unbridled anger, 'you ordered the murder of my parents—Gary and Kay Darlington. Do you remember them?'

The man answered softly while still clutching his wounded leg, 'Yes, they needed to be made an example of.'

David growled and barked back, 'You orphaned me and your goons destroyed my face. I'm going to be a little generous with you and let you have a painless death. But only if you tell me who were those two goons that attacked my family were and where they are now.'

It was the first time that the two boys saw someone accept their fate. Thompson, in his blood-covered silk robe, took a deep breath and answered softly, 'I had them executed. They were planning to overthrow me.'

David believed him.

It was a grave moment as Akira watched David place the revolver in Thompson's mouth. The man felt himself slip into an abyss of despair; the last thing he saw was the boy with the monstrous face pulling the trigger.

seven

'I GUESS HE took our advice,' Hult told Lomax.

A massive scene had assembled along a railway line that led north from the Outer London Boroughs.

It was a grim day with bleak weather. This, along with a bloody death, created the perfect atmosphere for the two Chief Superintendents.

The railway had been stopped as the authorities had found the body of a tall Japanese man with unusually long arms. The man was dressed in a vintage pin-stripe brown suit accompanied by a matching pinstripe brown fedora. He had been shot twice in the back and then had his throat slit. A gruesome but quick kill.

The body had been discovered by a teenage couple attempting to elope. Discovering a dead body so soon into their journey into the real world had made them change their minds, much to the relief of their parents.

The boy, who had been the one to spot the body, was quite horrified. Not because of the body's condition. But he was horrified because of just how long and odd the dead man's arms were. It looked unnatural, almost mutated.

The eloping couple had quickly called emergency services

and were smart to request the police and coroner. The girl knew who a coroner was; all the detective novels she had read as a child had been of use. When the police arrived at the scene, the local constables had foolishly decided to question the poor teenagers for several hours. Based on who the man was, it was extremely unlikely that this was done by anyone other than a professional.

After getting confirmation of the man's identity through a facial scan, Lomax and Hult had to take a break from their Champagne celebration, courtesy of their recently acquired ten thousand pounds, and take a call from a distant police precinct that the man they were hunting had conveniently wound up dead yet again. It seemed to be a frequent occurrence for the pair but no one, not even internal affairs, would dare to question the antics of Scotland Yard's two most well-reputed detectives.

The drive from Scotland Yard to the scene of the crime had been a long and hastily plotted one. Fortunately, the two Chief Superintendents did quite enjoy driving their Chrysler 300. The countryside also turned out to be quite the pleasant change from the boring drabness of London.

Upon arrival, Lomax and Hult were slightly surprised to see over two dozen people around the body.

'It is because of his arms,' explained a posh Frenchman travelling through the area. 'They are exquisite.'

Hult had laughed hearing that.

Assistant Commissioner Hooter had arrived before them. Lomax couldn't help but jealously cuss Hooter under his breath. The man had access to the police helicopter as and when he pleased; an inefficient but ego-boosting use of precious resources.

Before the two Chief Superintendents even got to see the body, the Assistant Commissioner approached them and barked sarcastically, 'Thanks for showing up, boys. We really enjoyed waiting for you because of all that time we have to spare.'

Lomax flashed Hooter a dirty look.

The Assistant Commissioner continued, 'We've confirmed the identity. It's Kenta Saito. But given his reputation, I don't understand why someone would kill him or even managed to.'

'Well, that's why you hire us,' Hult's words decimated Hooter.

Pushing their useless boss aside and then fighting their way through the crowd, Hult and Lomax finally got to see the body for themselves. But they had to hide their smiles; there were too many people around who didn't fully understand their venomous nature.

'Well this is definitely Saito,' Hult remarked.

'How could it not be? Look at how long those goddamn arms are.'

'No wonder he was a master assassin. He could use his bloody arm as a noose,' Hult joked.

Hooter approached the two Chief Superintendents from behind and asked, 'So, first impressions?'

'Well, not a very good one. He's not that talkative and I'm not a big fan of the shy type.'

Hooter barked, 'Have some respect when you talk to me Lomax. I'm the Assistant Commissioner for god's sake.'

Lomax retorted, 'Sir, I promise I'll be nicer if you actually become the Commissioner. You're not very threatening as the Assistant. Respect is for a person, not a rank. It needs to be earned like everything else.'

The Assistant Commissioner grew red. He was about to have a go at Lomax when Hult put his arm on the man and gave him a calming look. Hooter considered it for a second and realized Lomax was right. With that thought, he retreated into the crowd.

'I bet his suit is custom made,' Hult hypothesized looking at the body again.

'Why?' asked Lomax.

'Well, I'm quite sure no one manufacturers suits with that arm-length for the general public,' Hult spoke coolly.

Kenta Saito was dead on the ground. His life had ended by being shot and stabbed in the first-class coach of a train and being thrown onto the English countryside like an unwanted bag of manure. The legendary master assassin's end had been as disastrous as the countless manhunts to catch him. Maybe he deserved better but he probably didn't. His life may have meant something in the land of the rising sun but here in the fields of British harvest, he was just another dead piece of hunk interrupting the day.

The Ambition of Sam Winterfield

one

*I*N A SMALL office that belonged seemingly to the head of the business, Sam and Victor sat facing an empty chair. Amy and Michael were always excluded when the matter was one of revenge. The man they had come to meet had temporarily left the room for what was explained to be an urgent phone call and neither of the two men seemed particularly impressed by the situation.

It was about six in the evening and Sam was growing impatient. He wanted to go home and watch a film with Amy like he did every night. Breaking routine seemed almost criminal to him. Victor, on the other hand, understood Sam's restlessness and was not happy with the way the person they had come to see was behaving.

Shutter & Black Investigators was officially a private investigation agency. It was the kind of place a husband would visit to get the dirt on his cheating wife or a businessman would visit to find out who was stealing expensive office supplies. Unofficially, Shutter & Black often had no time to do such work and dealt with a much more expensive commodity: information.

The entire business was handled by just two men and it

had been difficult to explain to the authorities just how they had managed to mint so much in such little time while doing nothing illegal. Their office was just a single floor in the Rudd Building in downtown London. It was difficult to meet either Simon Shutter or Carter Black without a prior appointment but Victor had been lucky enough to take advantage of his life-long companionship with Simon. The man came a long way since being the son of a corner-shop owner and had upgraded from a cheap Volkswagen to the Range Rover standing outside.

Simon returned to the room, pocketing his phone. He looked apologetically towards Victor and Sam as he settled into the seat across them. Before anything, he reached out and shook Sam's hand and graciously said, 'It's a pleasure to finally meet you, Mr Winterfield. Victor has spoken highly of you for quite some time.'

Victor thought that Simon may have crossed a line but he would rather no one be in their comfort zone than all of them basking in the safety of familiarity.

'Victor tells me that you may be able to help us, Mr Shutter,' Sam spoke formally. He was in no mood for anything that wasn't business.

Simon Shutter smiled and then explained softly, 'Payment first; information later.'

Sam looked at Victor, who then went ahead and pushed an envelope towards the dealer. A discount had been negotiated already.

Simon spent three long minutes counting the money. It was clear that he didn't trust anyone and no one ever questioned that about him.

'It's all there,' smiled Shutter as he placed the money in the drawer of the wooden desk in front of him.

Sam was getting impatient. He spoke bluntly, 'How are you going to help me kill this man, Mr Shutter?'

Simon smiled. He then took a long breath and chose his words carefully, 'It took me a long time but I have managed to find a man matching the loose description you gave me. I have yet to decipher his name but he has definitely been seen multiple times around the Winterfield Estates Office and SkyStar Project four years ago. It seems that the man has worked hard to remain in the shadows but in London no one can hide from me. He's currently residing within The Kitano Club and has been paying Akira Kitano a lot of money for protection. I also believe that it is those funds that have been used by The Kitano Gunmen to acquire and redistribute the new Echelon Drug on the streets.'

Sam grimaced. His life couldn't begin until he ended his parents' murderer, but to take on one of London's two biggest crime syndicates? That was a war that a fourteen year old and his chauffeur were unlikely to win. Victor too had a grave scowl plastered across his face. He had hoped that the revenge would be quick and tense. He wanted the boy to get some solace from the crippling burden that had endlessly plagued his life. Now it seemed the solution would be much more complicated.

'How do you suggest I proceed?' Sam asked.

'Well, Mr Winterfield, you may not have an army but you do have one big fat bank account. There's no problem in this world that can't be solved without money. I know a lot about The Kitano Gunmen and The Forge Mobsters. They're ruthless and all they crave is blood and cash. First, I would suggest gently approaching Akira Kitano and offering him a big fat lump sum to resolve the matter himself. Taking a big paycheck to kill a man they're protecting would seem like too golden an opportunity to pass up. It would be the easiest money he could earn. However, if he does turn out to have a shred of honour, you'll need to approach The Forge boss, David Darlington, and pay him enough to go to war with The Kitano Gunmen and take out the man they're protecting.'

Sam was not happy with the solution. Starting a Mob bloodbath in London was not the ideal way to spend his summer vacation but if that's what it would come down to, he was more than willing to do what needed to be done.

two

On this night, there was a long queue outside The Forge as coked up youngsters craved to get in on the thumping music inside. Two visibly armed bouncers would ensure that the quality and quantity of the crowd was appropriately regulated. The weapons they carried to do their job, however, seemed a bit overpowered. One wielded a Mossberg 590A1, while the other carried a Hawk 12.

The two bouncers had dealt with a lot in their lives but what came next even surprised them a little. A white Rolls Royce Phantom pulled up to the club and a young boy got out from the back seat. He was dressed in a sharp black suit with an open buttoned white shirt. He walked straight up to the bouncer exuding confidence and spoke coldly, 'I'm Sam Winterfield and I'm here to see David Darlington.'

The bouncer couldn't even believe that a fourteen year old had the guts to walk up to a shotgun wielding guard and demand something of him. But looking at the car he had arrived in, he realized that money bought a lot of things and one of them was confidence.

David Darlington's office walls were soundproofed so that business was not disturbed by the thumping bass of deep house music. He lay back in a black leather chair with his hat hanging low across his face. The disfigurement was mostly hidden except for the little burns across his lower left cheek. Unfortunately, no hat ever hung that low. At this age, he had learned use it to his advantage to intimidate. When a bit younger, it had cost him a social life and expensive prices from even the lowliest prostitutes.

Sitting across the man who had spent a large part of his life leading London's major mob syndicate was a little fourteen year old brat that went by the name of Sam Winterfield. Not one Forge mobster guarding the building failed to be surprised by this little boy being escorted through the club. Even David Darlington himself had only agreed to meet him out of raw curiosity.

Sam had been afraid but now he seemed to have regained control of the situation. It was just him and this hideous man across him. Now, it was just a negotiation like the ones in the movies. Both sides had something to offer and a settlement could be reached. But no matter how his mind tried to rationalize it, there was a growing fear within him. He had seen one too many guns in the past few minutes to feel even remotely safe.

'Do you know who I am?' asked Darlington.

'I could ask you the same question,' answered Sam.

The mob boss was not impressed. He lifted his hat to reveal the rest of his deformed face and looked closer towards the boy.

'I'm Mr Darlington, little boy, and I'm the leader of one of London's most dangerous organizations. So if you want to keep your head I would suggest you stop playing games.'

Sam was surprised, 'You'd kill a fourteen-year old like me?'

'Women, children, everyone—we don't discriminate. We kill everyone.'

The little boy frowned. He was now a bit worried but managed to keep his cool. 'That's perfect, Mr Darlington. You seem like the kind of man I was hoping for.'

The mob boss gave a confused look. 'I like you, kid. What can I do for you?' he said.

'Well, Mr Darlington,' began Sam, 'my parents were executed in front of my eyes four years ago by a man whose name or identity I do not know. I was ten back then and let me tell you, it's not the kind of thing anyone lets go.'

'So, you're an orphan?' interrupted Darlington.

'Yes...' murmured Sam.

'Well, at least we've got something in common. Go on.'

Sam didn't know how to react to such information but continued anyway, 'I've tried to forgive and forget, but I don't want to. I want that man dead, and his family if he has one. No one should be allowed to take away something from me and allowed to live happily ever after. It's not fair.'

'The world's not fair,' Darlington was harsh.

Sam grew red but tried to maintain his composure. He then continued, 'I want what I want, Mr Darlington, and I hope that you will help me get it. I have recently received information that the killer of my parents is being protected by Akira Kitano and The Kitano Club. I would like to pay you to attack them and bring this man to me, dead or alive.'

'How much would you pay?'

'One million pounds.'

David Darlington struggled with temptation. 'I can't, Sam.

The Forge and The Kitano Club agreed on a truce just last night. It's stupid to be fighting each other when we've got bloody Scotland Yard to deal with. I'm sorry, boy. I know revenge needs to be fulfilled. Have you tried just offering Akira money to bump off the guy himself? You can buy his loyalty and a lot more for a million quid.'

Sam looked down in despair. He hadn't expected this. 'Yes, I actually did offer Kitano money. He said that the killer had offered him something a lot more exciting.'

David Darlington and Sam Winterfield stared at each other.

three

Sam stepped out of the club and was once again greeted with an onslaught of looks and gazes by the people in line waiting to get in.

One of the younger men towards the back of the queue shouted to the bouncer, 'Kids come here? What kind of joke are you running?'

The bouncer with the shotgun shouted back, 'Shut the hell up and wait your turn like everybody else.'

Sam walked to the road with a look of disappointment on his face. His car pulled up and Victor opened the door. Sam got in without a word. Victor recognized that as a bad sign.

The car accelerated and headed back towards the mansion. Victor was worried and asked carefully, 'So, did you get to meet Mr Darlington?'

'Yes,' replied Sam coldly.

Victor was curious. 'What's the man like?'

'Hideous.'

Victor decided not to push too hard and turned on the radio.

'I Saw Her Standing There' by The Beatles started playing.

Sam took a breath and decided to explain. 'He's ugly. His

face is rotten. I can see why it scares most people. It doesn't scare me though, I don't think anything scares me anymore. Even if there is something out there that I might be afraid of, it's definitely more than a man's face. David Darlington is probably a good man. I think he's just bitter. He runs the London Mob like a business. There were papers all over his office. I wasn't expecting that. He's an orphan too, you know? He told me. I think we bonded on that. I've never met another orphan before. It was unsettling and comfortable at the same time.'

'What did he say? Can he help?' Victor asked not knowing what kind of answer to hope for.

The song on the radio changed. 'All Day and All of the Night' by The Kinks started playing.

'Darlington and Kitano seemed to have reached a rather sudden agreement. Their war has ended. I offered him a lot but it seemed like no amount of money would change the man's mind. It was the same issue we had with Kitano. It seems as though the two men are more similar than we thought.'

'So, he can't go after the killer?' Victor asked.

'No, there is no way he'll attack The Kitano Club. He did do me one favour though. He didn't ask for anything in return. He said he understood an orphan's revenge.'

'What was the favour?' Victor asked gliding the car through traffic.

'He said that even though he couldn't go after him himself, he would call up Akira Kitano and ensure that the killer was released from Kitano's protection as a part of the truce. At least that way we still have a shot at attempting to take him out. He said it was the least he could do for a fellow orphan.'

Sam ended his explanation emotionally. He found it odd that he felt closer to David Darlington than anyone else in his life. It was strange how the most unusual people could find themselves attached to one another.

'I'm The Wolf' by Howlin' Wolf started playing on the radio.

The Loyalty of Fasial Haseem

one

THE OLD MAN cruised through Soho in a sparkling black Aston Martin One 77. Many people made the mistake of believing that luxury was only correlated with expense. This was quite far from the truth. The car shuffled slowly through narrow crowded roads and while it was one hell of a gorgeous vehicle, it blended in well with the night and didn't attract too much attention.

He pulled up in front of The Kitano Club and parked in one of the VIP spots. One of the bouncers to the establishment came running towards the vehicle as the VIP spots had to be reserved in advance and Old Man had done no such the thing. He got out of the vehicle and stared menacingly at the bouncer that approached him.

'Sir, I'm going to have to ask you to move your car,' the bouncer said. He was a well-built and fair-skinned man. His muscle had caused him to look laughably wild but his strong jaw and powerful structure was intimidating. His hair cut suggested that he may have been recently released from the Royal Armed Forces and his eyes gleamed with contact lenses.

He didn't respond with words and just handed the man two £50 notes.

The bouncer pocketed the money. He decided that it was probably best to call the person who had reserved the spot, a Mrs Rowan in a red Bentley, and alert her that the facility had been overbooked tonight.

The Old Man entered The Kitano Club and was the only person to not be frisked upon walking in. He just had an aura of importance about him that demanded to be treated differently and with fear. The hostess approached him. She was a young girl, her Estonian heritage and recent news reports suggested that she was probably a victim of human trafficking. She wore a short black dress, had short blonde hair and an average face that was doused with a bit too much make-up.

'What can I help you with, Sir?' She asked as politely as she could.

'Point me towards Akira Kitano,' the Old Man ordered in a cold voice.

The hostess was surprised at the man's abrupt nature but knew that it was beyond her pay scale to question it. She pointed towards a charming young Japanese man dressed in a black tuxedo doing his rounds and greeting all the guests at the tables.

As he watched closely, Akira caught the man's glaze. Seeing a destructive figure in an overcoat and fedora usually attracted one's curiosity and Akira decided that the rounds could be postponed for the night.

The leader of The Kitano syndicate approached him, 'What can I help you with today?' he asked.

He was quite charming for a mob boss.

'Not here,' he replied.

Akira Kitano nodded his head and then led the way to

a staircase in the back and up to his private office. The two men got seated and took a minute to get comfortable and study each other. Akira did not know what kind of deal to offer and the Old Man couldn't decide on how much to offer.

'So, what can I help you with?' Kitano asked coldly.

'Protection and anonymity,' he replied.

Akira explained sincerely, 'We're not that kind of organization. We work for ourselves. We're not goons to be hired.'

'If you were goons, I wouldn't be here.'

Akira took a moment and then asked the crucial question, 'Who the hell even are you?'

The Old Man wasn't a fan of the disrespect he had just been subjected to but decided to answer as unthreateningly as he could bring himself to. 'You may never know.'

Kitano didn't like to be at a severe lack of knowledge. His temper kicked in and he barked threateningly, 'I could just beat it out of you old man.'

'Would you really be stupid enough to try?' he retorted.

Akira leaned back in his chair. He was dealing with something else here. He wondered whether to proceed or to just a pop a bullet in this man's chest. But before anything, it was probably best to hear his offer, 'So, I give you protection and anonymity. What do you give me in return?'

'What everyone wants: money.'

Kitano shook his head, 'You could offer me 5 million quid and I wouldn't be interested. We have enough cash. You told me you were different, you're not.'

The Old Man tried again, 'I could also propose something unique.'

Akira was now interested. He leaned in, 'Like what?'

'Well, there is one thing from my previous life that I've kept hidden for quite some time. But now I can offer it to you as it serves no practical purpose in my life.'

Akira didn't say anything. He just waited patiently.

'It's an old Chinese Warship from the 1960s. It's parked a few miles off the south coast. You protect me and the ownership papers are yours.'

Akira Kitano smiled. This was just the kind of thing he was interested in. A legally owned old warship in international waters? The opportunities were endless.

The two men shook hands. He was to stay in a special room within The Kitano Club itself and his Aston Martin One 77 would be secured in Akira's personal garage.

There was one thing that still needed to be cleared.

'Who are we protecting you from?' asked Akira.

He flashed a look of momentary concern through his mask of fear and answered, 'The people of London.'

The man's answer was vague but instantly understood by Kitano. He was referring to a headline that had plagued the newspapers lately, 'The people of London want justice.' It referred to the murder of Mayor George Heartwood and the lack of even a suspect in the investigation of his death.

two

THE ENGLISH CHANNEL is the arm of the Atlantic Ocean that separates England and France. A medium-sized rotten old fishing boat battled the rough seas and headed south. It was a green-blue coloured vessel named *The Penance of Arthur*. While only designed to house eight workers, it currently was home to a total of thirteen people which put pressure on the ship's ability to provide. The ship's crew hadn't even been allowed onto the journey as no fishing was involved. It was the just the owner of the boat and a dozen mobsters in fancy black suits.

Visibility was almost non-existent as the boat motored through the waves. The captain was doing his best to maintain stability but there would still be the rough and high waves were not doing anyone any favours. Sitting on the deck was supposed to help the mostly sea-sick mobsters, but the occasional splash of ice-cold salt water kept worsening their condition.

It had been an eventful journey. One of the hoods had almost gone overboard as he stood at the side of the boat vomiting into oblivion. That, coupled with the instability of the boat, and a sudden large wave knocked the man off of his feet and nearly into the cold depths of the sea. As much as the mob was about brotherhood and survival, the current situation probably meant that they wouldn't have even considered stopping and retrieving him.

The Captain of the ship was a man named Phillip Stein. But everyone he knew simply called him 'Pop'. He couldn't remember how the nickname had caught on and something told him that he probably didn't want to.

The Captain was an old man with a thick head of white hair and a fat white beard. He was a little chubby and wore drab red overalls covering a green t-shirt. He was just a man who enjoyed the sea and had done well in converting his fishing hobby into his occupation.

Like many other men, the reason for this endeavour into the ocean had come from one tangible and tempting source: thousands of pounds in cash. He had been a bit worried when he saw a dozen men in suits and fedoras approaching him but when they made their intentions clear, all he could think about was the money. They had offered him twenty thousand pounds for the job. That kind of cash could allow him to retire much earlier than expected. But the money had bound him to silence and that was probably something that could cause trust issues in the future with his crew.

There was only one reason that the London Mob usually went to sea: to dump bodies. Twelve men to do the job may even suggest a mass ocean grave. Fortunately, it had been made clear to Pop that such was not the case. They were out 'scouting' a location and anything that they found must remain a secret. Pop did not enjoy the vagueness but he understood the terms.

Paul Harrison was the leader of the twelve Kitano Gunmen on board *The Penance of Arthur*. When Akira Kitano himself had assigned him the job, Paul had been excited for the adventure on the sea, especially when he was explained what he was looking for. But when he saw his men puke and suffer for countless hours at the mercy of the motion, he realized that such was not the case.

Paul was a musician turned muscleman for The Kitano Club. He was a whiz with the guitar and was actually a successful performer before an unfortunate run-in with The Forge led to some broken fingers and wasted talent. Pledging revenge, he signed on with The Kitano Club to tear London to shreds.

Akira Kitano had done well in ordering no less than twelve men to go on this mission. He had made sure that the men didn't know each other well and there was a severe lack of trust in the group, so that there was no chance of them combining forces against him. After all, what he had sent them after could be his greatest prize from the unlikeliest of sources.

Paul currently sat on the cold deck clutching his coat close to him. He watched the pale faces of the men under his command and wondered whether this might've been the most eccentric endeavour by the London Mob in recent history. They had gone down to Portsmouth without the slightest bit of planning and with only the coordinates of their destination in hand. However, with the amount of cash they were offering, it was unlikely that they would have difficulty in finding someone who would agree to transport them.

Paul slowly rose from the deck and approached the little

cabin within which the boat's controls rested. Pop was inside manning the wheel and making sure that they didn't lose speed.

'How much further?!' Paul asked Pop, screaming over the noise. According to the last update almost half an hour ago, the Captain had clearly said that they were almost there. The finality of the situation drew close. The suffering of the mobsters would hope to reveal a lasting reward.

Pop smiled at Paul's question. He didn't respond with words but simply pointed ahead. Paul turned to look at the distant horizon. The prize was finally in sight.

All the mob-members rose to see what they had come to find.

In the distance, a large Chinese Warship from the 60s rested gallantly on the ocean. It had been stripped of its weaponry but was still an intimidating sight, as big as a container-ship. The top was flat, not unlike the large air-craft carriers that had runways for planes, but this magnificent vessel was not owned by some massive well-funded government. It was owned by a bunch of conniving men that ran brothels and sold drugs on street-corners.

The Chinese Warship was of the Crusader Class had been given the name *Bruce*. It rested peacefully with its anchor deep in the sea floor. The large waves which had been thrashing the little fishing boat couldn't even be felt by a vessel so magnificent and imposing. But what was disturbing was the total absence of life on-board *Bruce*. It was a ghost ship waiting to be taken over. Paul and the rest of The Kitano Gunmen could only speculate as to what Akira planned to do with such a glorious asset.

three

'THEY'RE JUST LOOKING for any excuse to make us work, aren't they?' Lomax asked Hult. The two men stood at the docks surrounded by the usual two dozen people that swarmed the scene every time a murder took place in London.

It was a cold day. The sun was covered up by clouds and the sky was the tradition London grey. Birds were drowned out by the rumbling of engines in the distance and tall buildings obscured the sky. The atmosphere smelt of wealth and sweat.

Lomax had volunteered to drive the two down from Scotland Yard when he was called to the scene. The phone call itself had been an unusual one; an unknowing constable who had been ordered to inform the relevant people. The investigators, or in this case the Chief Superintendents, were never the first call. If either Hult or Lomax were asked to guess, they would both put their money on Assistant Commissioner Hooter getting the first call and then letting him decide which men to bring onto the job.

The drive from Scotland Yard to the docks had been a quick one. Lomax and Hult had fully utilized their privilege to blow the siren on top of their Chrysler 300 and ignore all traffic laws. It was almost that their maturity was temporarily inhibited as the two men would deliriously speed through London roads threatening the lives of those that they had taken an oath to protect.

Arriving at the scene, the two Chief Superintendents had quickly been taken to the body.

An old man lay on the pavement. There was a bullet wound in the middle of his forehead and it was clear that he had been fished out from the Thames. He was dressed in red overalls with a non-threatening face. If he had been alive, both the cops would have probably assumed that he was a jolly fellow.

Assistant Commissioner Hooter approached the two men and put one arm on each of their shoulders to signify camaraderie. The two Chief Superintendents quickly shuffled off the partial embrace uncomfortably.

'How on earth is this a case for Diplomatic Affairs?' Hult asked. He really didn't need his time wasted.

'This is just a local murder. Why drag us into this? Are you running that low on manpower? You could've just requested us. No need to disguise the investigation,' Lomax chipped in.

Assistant Commissioner Hooter had been expecting the reaction. He said, 'It is a Diplomatic Affairs case. The man had just sailed in from international waters. That technically implies that it's your department. Especially so, if he was killed there and then the body was brought back.'

'There is absolutely no chance of that. If they had killed him out in the sea then they would've dumped him there. He was shot upon the completion of his trip.'

'Good analysis,' said Hooter 'That's why I need you handling this. The department's performance has dipped.'

Hult growled in frustration. He had walked into the other man's trap. Hult and Lomax might've been the investigative talent but Hooter was king of office politics.

The Assistant Commissioner left the scene. Lomax used his hand to motion for the Chief Constable waiting patiently on the side to come over.

The Chief Constable, the plainest and most uninteresting man Lomax and Hult had ever seen, approached them and stood at attention. His formal attitude was unnerving. He clearly didn't understand that such behaviour was only necessary when they were being watched by outsiders.

'Prelim,' Hult said. He was referring to the preliminary report that the Chief Constable should have collected upon arrival at the scene.

The Chief Constable cleared his throat and recited what he had clearly rehearsed in the past few minutes, 'The body was discovered this morning by the local dockworkers. They had instantly called and reported in and provided no basis for suspicion. It took about two hours to get the body out in proper condition by the analysts. Locals confirmed that his name was Phillip Stein. However, no one used his name in conversation and he was mostly just referred to as Pop. Last night, there was a lot of commotion in the area when twelve men in black suits and fedoras approached different fishermen and boat owners demanding to be taken out to a specific location out in international waters. They were confirmed to be mobsters as many guns were sighted but we are unsure as to whether they worked for The Forge, The Kitano Club or were unaffiliated.'

'No one in London is unaffiliated.' Lomax interrupted.

The Chief Constable hesitated and pointed to the fishing boat nearby. He then continued his report, 'That is Pop's fishing vessel and is named *The Penance of Arthur*. It was using that that Pop transported the twelve mobsters out to sea and brought them back sometime in the late hours of the night in return for a large sum of money.'

'What's your guess, Chief?' Hult asked the Chief Constable.

The man looked at Hult and did his best to formulate an effective hypothesis, 'Sir, I'd say that the men probably took the boat out to dump a body or drugs. When they got back, the mobsters simply decided to kill the man instead of paying him in order to not spend any cash.'

'It was a good attempt but you've got to delve deeper. These mobsters don't lack for money. The London syndicates are notorious for that. They're minting cash faster than they can launder it. It would've been much easier to pay Pop off. I think the real reason is bit more interesting. These men were looking for something and they found it. They couldn't have trusted Pop with the secret of their discovery and had to let him go. Is the fishing vessel's navigation still online? We should be able to check their travel log and discover where they went.'

The Chief Constable shook his head, 'No sir, it's completely destroyed. They fired an entire clip into the machinery.'

Hult smiled. It was just as he had expected.

four

A GENERATION AGO, THE grandest construct in the whole of the Shah's Empire had been designed by young Faisal himself. It was a massive structure sprawling over dozens of acres and had been built in just a year on the order of the Shah. Gold plating overwhelmed any visitor, of which there were few, and the white marble that covered the floor often ran red with blood.

The castle was perched on a hill at such a height that one required a car to reach. It was physically impossible to reach the palace by ascending the several hundred steps that had been constructed; such demanding endeavours were rarely attempted in a nation where people died of hunger and thirst every waking day.

Within the Holy Room of the Imperial Palace, the Shah met the young Faisal one day.

The Holy Room was the Shah's usual place of business. It was a grand room with thirty foot high ceilings and four grand pillars along the edges. The Shah's throne rested a dozen feet above the ground on a large red podium so there was plenty of room for him to look down upon the commoners. It was a huge assembly where dozens of his subjects would gather every morning to inform and entertain. It was where the big decisions were announced and televised, and where traitors to the Shah were executed and displayed.

Faisal had spent countless hours in the room, but this moment was unlike any other. The Shah rested on his grand throne and at his feet was Faisal on his knees. He clutched the dictator's hand as it was placed upon his head.

The Shah was a young man that commanded an enormous amount of fear and respect. He was just thirty-five but he ruled with the force and experience of a man with the wisdom of generations. He was handsome and sharp. Today, however, his face held a look of disdain and despair. He was not happy and the fact that he had the Commander of his Secret Police trembling at his feet made him feel even more insecure.

'Look at me Faisal and get on your feet,' the Shah spoke.

The young man adhered to his master's wishes and rose.

The end was here. The Shah's empire had been fending off the British Forces for almost a week but their army was much stronger and had easily broken through. Missiles and bombs had wrecked the lands and the rivers ran red with the blood of the soldiers. The Englishmen had come and conquered with supreme rapidity. After hourly advancements, they had made their way to the capital and soon would be knocking on the doors of the Imperial Palace. There was no solitude now and there hadn't been for weeks. All one would hear were the rapid gunshots of assault rifles and the crippling impacts of British Artillery.

'We can still get you out, My Lord. I shall act as a decoy while you escape,' Faisal offered in desperation.

'Don't be foolish. It is better that I die with pride rather than live without.'

'I will defend you with my dying breath. Just as I had taken an oath to,' the young commander promised.

The Shah shook his head, 'You're much too intelligent for such behaviour, Faisal. My end is inevitable but I have something important for you to do. I want you to escape with the British Forces as part of their rescue mission. Go to their English homeland and settle well. After a few weeks, I want you to head down to the coordinates I am about to give you. In that area, you will find a gift that the Chinese had given me in return for our oil. It is an old warship.'

'A warship?'

The Shah smiled and confirmed, 'Yes, a warship. It is stripped of weaponry but is anchored in the sea. I don't care what you do with the ship itself, it is what is in the captain's cabin of the vessel that matters. There is a singular document that holds the identity of a woman. I want you to find her and kill her.'

Faisal was confused. 'Who is she?' he asked.

'She is the love of my life,' the Shah explained, 'and I want you to send her to me in heaven. She escaped abroad when we were young and the uprising began, but I had a man track her down and hide the details of her new identity on the warship.'

It was a difficult for moment for Faisal as he pondered his Shah's wishes. The British Forces would enter the palace any second now and he needed to tell his master whether he planned on completing his final mission or not. He knew it was arrogant of his master to believe that he could united with his long lost loved one in heaven, but Faisal understood that a man about to face death was usually more inclined to be optimistic.

The commander took a bow and responded with his hand on his heart, 'It shall be done, My Shah.'

The dictator was glad. He could now finally rest in peace knowing that he would in time be reunited with the person whose departure had left a gaping hole within him, something that had led to the ambition required to conquer and stabilize a nation of turmoil.

The Shah took a deep breath, 'Give me peace. I shall not suffer this indignity at a foreign hand.'

He followed his master's wishes and retrieved his Luger P08 pistol. The Shah closed his eyes as the commander aimed the gun at his ruler's heart and pulled the trigger.

five

THE OLD MAN stood on a cold London road. Faisal hadn't taken long in adopting the fedora and overcoat after arriving in England. He felt too vulnerable without it. This was not his home. These people were not his friends. He needed to be guarded and the only man he trusted was himself.

A grey sky overwhelmed the horizon. Rain poured heavily, scattering the few people daring to go outside and be pelted by it. Cars sped down the narrow lanes attempting to reach their destinations as soon as possible, taxi drivers gave up and pulled up to cafes and restaurants. The Old Man stood unfazed, staring at his objective.

Pemberton Estate was a sprawling home in central London. Only few families such as the Winterfields and the Pembertons could afford such luxuries. The home was heavily guarded. There were electrified fences and multiple CCTV cameras. Oddly enough, there were no actual people guarding the premises. Only a fool would dare to trust technology alone.

Nigel Pemberton, the owner of Pemberton Mansion, was a big player in the stock market and had recently been in the newspaper for successfully exposing and shorting against a massive Ponzi scheme. He was a handsome man and a local hero. But he was not home and it wasn't him that the man was interested in.

Nigel Pemberton had recently married a woman a few years older than him. He had said that it had been love at first sight; claims of her being a huntress after his money were quickly squashed. The woman, who now went by the name of Antonia Pemberton, was a lady with a dark past that had unfortunately been uncovered.

The Old Man had been surprised when he had first laid his eyes upon the warship a few months ago. His master had held such a powerful asset and never mentioned it to anyone; it seems his need to protect had overcome his arrogance.

It hadn't been easy to get onto the vessel and even more difficult to actually find and retrieve the document that had been placed in the captain's cabin. Uncovering the information he had been impressed by how well Antonia had managed to hide her past. She had done everything from taking English lessons to make her sound more British to cosmetic surgery to mask her original bronze skin-tone.

But no longer did any of that matter.

He approached the door of the mansion and pressed the buzzer. It was a full minute before Antonia responded, 'Who are you?'

With his face masked behind his fedora he replied, 'The Boss has sent something for you.'

She didn't even consider him a threat. Maybe she had lost her edge after all these years.

The door swung open and the Old Man entered. He walked along a short path lined by beautifully landscaped grass on both sides and fifteen-foot high trees along the ends. He arrived at the door and pressed a little marble bell along the left wall.

It was just one glimpse of his face with a certain kind of sadomasochistic smile seen though the gap between his collar and fedora that put the fear inside her, but it was too late for her to retreat to safety.

The Old Man didn't say a word. He just used his arms and leapt for the woman's throat. His icy bare hands gripped her neck and he thrust her to the ground. He was quite sure that he was under surveillance, but it didn't matter. His face had been covered the whole time.

He pummelled Antonia against the ground as he watched her face go red and her life force flow out of her. His eyes were steely and cold while hers grew a warm red. She moaned but it was barely audible and with her scarce breaths, she managed to ask, 'Why?'

He succumbed as he continued to choke her and replied, 'For the Shah.'

Antonia managed to smile as she heard those words. She may have escaped her past but there was no doubt that she still treasured it.

He let his hands loosen as the woman stopped struggling and lay lifeless on the floor. He used his fingers to close her eyelids, a rare gesture of respect.

As he walked out of and away from the mansion, he felt a sense of relief. He had waited exactly to this day to complete his task. It had felt ceremonious to go through with his master's final wish on the anniversary of his death. But more importantly, he now felt free. He was no longer bound to the laws and ethics of his old empire. His duty and that part of his life were now in the past. It was time for him to rise up and conquer a kingdom of his own.

The Retribution of David Darlington

one

It was a warm evening as Sam and Amy walked out of the cinema. The show had ended almost at midnight, but teenagers like them were not new to such late nights. For Sam and Amy, school was not the demanding institution as it was for others.

The film was a romantic comedy about a boy struggling to find a good balance between the girl he loved and his passion for street racing. The standard fare of over-the-top jokes and silly clichés, but Amy wanted to see it and Sam had agreed. The two loved going to the cinema but it was mostly Amy; she realized that it was the only time Sam would forget his troubles and be engrossed enough to actually enjoy himself.

The two walked slowly down the road hand in hand, smiling at each other. Victor had parked the Rolls Royce Phantom just down the block.

The night sky grew darker and the air was misty. These were the more desolated areas of London but the facility to book private screenings was the reason why Amy had picked the place. She knew that Sam would be more comfortable.

The mood took a turn when they heard a cackle of drunk laughter coming down the alley ahead. Sam instantly put his jacket around Amy.

Two tall men came out of the alley and walked towards Sam and Amy. The tall men wore black suits and had dirty faces. It was quite likely that they were from the mob. They carried a bottle of cheap whiskey each and one could smell the alcohol and vomit on them from a distance.

Sam and Amy stopped walking, hoping that the two mobsters would simply ignore them and walk away. However, one of them saw Amy's pretty face and drew the attention of the other to her. As they approached her, Sam noticed the pistols within their coats.

Amy held onto Sam tightly. Sam too trembled with uncertainty. As strong and mature as he was, there was little he could do in such a situation.

'Well, you two really shouldn't be out here alone,' the uglier mobster said drunkenly.

'We'll be on our way,' Amy retorted quickly.

The two tried to move past but the mobsters blocked their way.

'Don't interrupt when men are talking,' the shorter mobster barked.

Sam was angry. He didn't want anyone talking to her like that. Much to Amy's surprise, he asked the mobster, 'Can I have a sip of your whiskey?'

The uglier mobster got confused but handed Sam the bottle.

Sam took the cap off the fragile glass bottle and then whispered into Amy's ear, 'Run.'

The girl quickly sprinted aside towards their car. Sam, on the other hand, gathered all his might and smashed the bottle of whiskey against the head of the shorter mobster. The man felt hundreds of little shards of glass pierce his face as blood covered his vision. He stumbled to the ground.

The other mobster dropped his bottle of whiskey and reached for his gun. Sam had almost accepted his fate; all he had wanted was to get Amy to safety.

The drunken mobster aimed his pistol loosely at Sam and murmured, 'You made a big mistake, kid.'

Before he could fire his gun, there was a roar of an engine behind him. The mobster turned around to see the white Rolls Royce Phantom ram into him, sending his body tumbling through the air. Sam dived out of the way but quickly managed to get back on his feet.

Victor pulled the car off the sidewalk and back onto the street. The two mobsters lay on the floor hurt but not dead.

'Sam! Let's get out of here! There could be more of them,' Amy shouted from the car.

Sam didn't want to simply run away. He walked over to the mobsters and picked up the uglier one's pistol. It was heavier and more rusted than he had expected but it didn't matter as long it got the job done.

The two beaten men looked up at the fourteen year old with fear.

In his drunken and damaged state, one of them managed to speak, 'Please don't. We weren't going to hurt you.'

Sam didn't care. He took aim and fired two rounds into the skull of the first mobster and then two in the face of the second. London echoed with the sound of the gunshots. A pool of blood formed at Sam's feet. Amy and Victor watched silently. Sam put the gun in his waistband and walked to the car. He sat in the back next to Amy as she looked at him with horror and fear. Victor put the car into motion and drove away from the scene.

Sam looked unnerved and simply said to his love, 'I'm sorry.'

two

Akira Kitano sat alone in his office, his face free of the false charm that he so generously employed. He was pondering the phone call he had just received. Over the years, the two crime syndicates would occasionally wrestle each other for territory and funds. People would die over disputes and cops would have to be paid off. It was just business. Never had Akira attempted to go after David's life or vice versa. At heart, they were still brothers and it would not be noble to mix business vendettas with private allegiances.

But today, David had called as his brother and made a request. A rich little orphan had come to his office demanding the life of the killer of his parents. It would've been foolish to go through with yet another war especially since no money was involved. The killer had to be released from Kitano's protection so that the boy could get his revenge without getting the syndicates involved.

But it was not that simple for Akira. The Old Man had not parted with money in exchange for protection, he had given Akira a gift much more prestigious. As the head of the Kitano Club, he was sure enough of himself to believe that if the Old Man had just paid him cash, he would be dead already and his body would be in the back of a car on the way to The Forge. That is how much Akira would be willing to do for his brother. But the gift of a warship had indebted the man.

Akira rose from his chair and walked out of the office. He headed towards the stairs that led to the loft where the Old Man had been residing. Upon reaching the door, he took a moment to gather himself and then knocked on the sturdy wood that blocked his path. A few minutes later, the door swung open and the man welcomed the Japanese mob boss into his humble abode.

The two men sat down on chairs facing each and looked at each other not knowing what to expect. It was always difficult to read the Old Man's expression; he always kept his face expertly hidden. But Kitano didn't care.

'An important favour has been called in and I'm afraid it's not to your advantage,' Akira spoke coldly.

The Old Man let out a soft disappointed sigh. 'Explain,' he said.

Kitano cleared his throat, 'I recently agreed to a truce with The Forge. As a part of that truce, there has been a special request to release you from my protection so that the syndicates do not get dragged into the conflicts of others.'

'I don't particularly care for Mob politics. I paid for a service and I expect it to be delivered,' the Old Man defended.

'The warship is a thing of beauty and that's the only reason you're not in the boot of a car with a bullet in your skull right now. Appreciate your second chance at life,' Akira spoke harshly and didn't wait for a reply. He simply rose from his seat and began to walk towards the door. His time was wasted arguing.

'Before you go, Mr Kitano, just tell me one thing,' said the Old Man.

'What?' asked Akira. His patience was running low.

'Did you say that this is being done as a favour to David Darlington?'

Akira turned around and looked him in the eye and answered clearly, 'Yes.'

'Well, I guess it must be difficult to refuse a request from your brother.'

Akira reached for his Colt 1911 but the Old Man leapt on him before he had the chance to draw out his gun.

Akira needed to kill this man before he told anyone; if the truth about him and David got out, they would be executed before they had the chance to explain. The two brothers had sacrificed countless lives for the sake of business.

Akira was on the floor. His arm went red as he used all of his strength to grab the pistol in his coat. The Old Man rested on top of him with one hand on his neck and the other preventing him from reaching the gun. The struggle lasted a few seconds, but Akira's strength was no match for the Old Man's lifetime of combat experience.

He wrapped his cold hands around the neck of the Japanese man and squeezed as hard as he could. This time, it wasn't just cold murder. He wanted revenge. He had been betrayed by the man to whom he had offered his greatest possession.

three

David Darlington stood in his bathroom. He was shirtless and wore only the thin cotton slacks that he had slept in. Even after all these years, he still hadn't gotten used to looking in the mirror every morning and believing that the monstrous thing that looked back at him was his own face. But at least it gave him the cold distance that allowed him to rule ruthlessly.

There was a knock on his bedroom door. This wasn't very unusual as many of his top enforcers had the key to his residence in case of emergencies. If he could trust them with his life then he could definitely trust them with his home.

'Come in,' he shouted.

The door swung open and a short chubby man in an expensive black suit walked in. He was sweating and looked tense. The man was Finch Kerrington, David's right hand man and most trusted advisor.

Looking at his boss's face without the cover of a fedora made even Kerrington uncomfortable and he averted his eyes. But his voice seemed to raise a graver cause of concern, 'Boss, I have some news.'

David looked at him sharply, Kerrington never spoke in riddles.

'What's wrong, Finch?' David asked.

The short henchman gulped and answered with worry, 'Sir, there were two encounters last night. Two of our men were shot dead near the Brix Cinema, and Akira Kitano was choked to death by the man he was protecting.'

David's face grew red. It took on a shape that looked much more monstrous than usual.

Kerrington failed to understand his boss's reaction. He had expected that he would be curious about who killed his men but uncontrollably joyous over the death of his long-term business rival. The city was now theirs for the taking. But something was wrong. No one had ever witnessed David Darlington so angry.

'I'll meet you at the office in an hour.' Darlington could barely maintain his composure.

Kerrington nodded and quickly left his boss's home.

David closed the door behind his little lieutenant and then fell to his knees. His arm gripped the table next to him and he wanted to scream with anger. Guilt overwhelmed him. Was it because of his request to get rid of the killer that Akira had died? It didn't matter. He had lost his brother and only the man who had taken him away could be held accountable.

But before he could consider revenge, a much more important matter took priority.

David reached for his phone and made a call. After a few seconds, there was an answer.

'Dad, I have some news,' he whispered to his father over the phone.

It was his son's tone that scared Ken Kitano more than anything else. He had always expected such a call but to actually face it was something that the man was not prepared to handle.

'What is it?' Ken Kitano asked, gathering every hope within him.

'Someone attacked Akira last night. He was choked to death,' David let out a tear as he actually said the words.

Ken Kitano did not respond.

David continued, 'I'm going to find whoever did it and I'm going to end them. I promise you…'

The phone call ended abruptly. His father had decided to discontinue the conversation to spare himself unrelenting pain. He had warned his sons that this day would come and facing its fruition was his greatest trial.

Darlington regained his composure. Today was the only day in his whole life when he was glad to possess such a monstrous face. He didn't need to be a human today. He just needed to be a force of anger that would not stop at anything to bring his brother to justice. But he would have to play it carefully with his syndicate. They could not know Darlington's true intentions as they would not understand why the mob boss would want to avenge the death of his enemy. But maybe, David pondered, they could be convinced with a presumptuous half-truth.

Later that day, the entirety of London underworld united under David Darlington. The remnants of The Kitano Club merged with The Forge in order to hunt down the man who had killed one of the most powerful men in the city. The mobsters came together under the same kind of schoolyard logic that siblings would apply to their behaviour. They may attack each other, but no bloody outsider could be allowed to attack them.

In this great city, there was no longer a bleak divide. However, the London Mob wasn't kind enough to offer a fair trial. Their system of justice simply let the man in charge decide just how much torture the offender would be put through before a painful death.

four

THE LOCAL CONSTABLES were placing the yellow tape around the crime scene when the black Chrysler 300 pulled up nearby. Lomax and Hult seemed their usual chipper selves with a lack of resentment for their Assistant Commissioner. This time, the man had decided not to lie to them.

The call that they had received that morning was a quick one. Considering the state of the city, however, Hult had done well to respect the chaos and play down the sarcasm. Hooter had informed the two men that the city was in a rage; the entire London Mob was out on a rampage looking for the killer of Akira Kitano. This had left Scotland Yard's manpower stretched quite thin and there was a double homicide near Brix Cinema that needed investigating. Considering how bored Hult and Lomax had become playing games on their phone all morning, it was agreed that a double homicide would be a pleasant and refreshing change of pace.

Upon arrival at the scene, Lomax had been quick to point out the lack of press. This was quite the blessing. Today, probably distracted by the Mob swarming the city in search of information, the reporters had more interesting stories to report.

The day was the usual London grey but at least it wasn't raining. But everything, from the walls to the pavement and even the roads, was coloured dark and brooding shades of black and grey. The two Chief Superintendents enjoyed the pleasant view, accentuated by the two dead bodies.

The two dead men were not recognizable by face because of the bullet wounds and their identities had been collected by checking their wallets.

'Who are they?' Lomax asked the leading constable on the scene.

The constable was just one of the regular constables who been put in charge as no Chief Constable was available. He was a muscular man, probably more brawn than brains.

'Two local mobsters, Sir,' answered the constable, 'Artie Russo and John Cunningham. They were out drinking at the local tavern last night when they…'

'Did you just say tavern?' Hult interrupted the constable. 'Who the hell says tavern?'

Lomax smiled and added in, 'I didn't realize we were in the 1800s. Are you going to tell me you arrived at the scene on a carriage?'

The constable was unnerved by the light-hearted and rude approach of the investigators.

Not knowing how else to respond, he continued, 'Well sir, they were at a local bar named The Great & Grand when they were asked to leave after having too much to drink. They headed down this way at which point they were murdered.'

'Who called it in?' asked Lomax.

'No one, sir,' responded the Constable. 'I drove past the victims on my daily rounds.'

The constable had been helpful, but not too helpful. Lomax & Hult shared a glance of understanding and then crouched down. It was time to figure out who would want to wipe out two lowly mobsters. Hult noticed the glass sticking out of one of the men's face and realized it was clearly not a premeditated event. Somebody had acted hastily and, considering that it was against mobsters, it probably meant self-defence.

Lomax was pursuing a different line of thought and turned to further question the constable, 'Were these two guys with Kitano or The Forge?'

'With The Forge, Sir,' the constable answered quickly and felt stupid for missing out such an important piece of information.

Hult rose to his feet and walked away from the two bodies and towards the cinema. The Brix Cinema had a small red glass door and Hult pushed it open to enter. The owner of the cinema, a middle-aged man behind the counter, was surprised to see the Chief Superintendent and asked, 'What can I help you with?'

'Do you have an electronic ticketing system?' Hult asked quickly.

The owner nodded in return and accessed his computer.

'The murder that took place down the street,' explained Hult, 'I believe it was committed by a person or multiple persons that were exiting your cinema. I need you to tell me what time the last show finished and a list of people who had purchased tickets.'

The owner spent a few minutes on his machine and then answered the Chief Superintendent unsurely, 'Sir, the last screening finished at around midnight. It was a private screening which was attended by only two of my regulars. I assure you they are not the killers. They wouldn't be able to murder mobsters even if they wanted to.'

'Who are they?' Hult asked impatiently.

'They're a young teenage couple—a rich lad by the name of Sam Winterfield, and his girlfriend Amy Burrows,' the owner spoke unsurely. He was quite fond of the two kids and needed them to keep his business afloat.

Hult instantly noticed the name Winterfield. He then realized that an opportunity such as this was probably better exploited for personal gain rather than being handed over to the Assistant Commissioner.

After all, the government didn't pay nearly as well as the mob for such information.

five

The Old Man sped down in his black Aston Martin One 77. He had not expected such a disastrous reaction when he had decided to end the life of Akira Kitano. For the first time in a long while, he felt vulnerable and scared in the face of real danger. He weaved in and out through cars, trying to put himself as far away from the incident as he could; his hunters were on the prowl and most of The Kitano Gunmen would recognize him or his car from a mile away.

The two mob syndicates had united surprisingly smoothly with the foot soldiers willing to pair up with one man from The Forge and one from The Kitano Club. David Darlington had explained this to be the most efficient way as only The Kitano Gunmen recognized the killer and The Forge Mobsters were better used rather than just waiting around all day. Not to mention that this teamwork would also make the transition from two separate syndicates into one overlord organization much simpler for Darlington in the future.

Unfortunately for the Old Man, his attempt to escape into anonymity was cut disastrously short when he took a turn and found himself surrounded by four pristine black Mercedes E240s

The four cars boxed in the Old Man's Aston Martin. Metal grinded and hideous noises sounded. They had been using The Kitano's helicopter to follow the car for quite some time and had placed groups of vehicles at all the possible turns that the man might take.

A huge crash took the four Mercedes E240s and the Aston Martin off road and into a building. Traffic stopped behind them and people scattered to the distance clutching their phones to record whatever was about to happen.

The Old Man wasn't wearing a seatbelt and had hit his head hard into the steering wheel. He was surrounded by four cars and each car had four men wielding heavy weapons. Out of the sixteen mobsters, the four in the front car were most likely dead on impact; it had been hit hardest in the crash.

But being familiar with conflict, the Old Man was the first to recover and quickly squeezed out the window of his Aston Martin and onto the top of the Mercedes on the right. He jumped off its top and dashed down the street. His overcoat fluttered in the wind and he had to use his hand to hold down his fedora on his head.

He looked back and was glad to see that none of the mobsters from the cars that had boxed him in were following after him. But the helicopter still lurked overhead and there were still a few thousand more men in black suits hunting him through the city.

He kept on running, his stamina and bursting adrenaline gave him the sensation of limitless energy, but he regretted not picking up a gun during his escape.

His weak sense of temporary safety was quickly shattered as three cars drifted out of a corner and drove towards him.

Two more Mercedes cars just like the ones that had crashed, but the one in the middle was a white BMW 720. The three cars pulled up in front of him. He dropped to his knees and hoped for mercy.

Four mobsters got out of black henchman vehicles. It was a full minute before the back door to the white BMW swung open and David got out. From the few onlookers that were close enough to see his face, there were nothing but gasps. The disfigured London Mob Boss had forgone his fedora today.

The Old Man looked at the man that approached him. Even though he had seen countless atrocities in his life, there were few that left a mark so deranged and dark as that of Darlington's disfigurement.

David walked up to the man. He had been surprisingly nimble and strong for someone of his age.

'Is this the man?' Darlington asked one of the henchmen from The Kitano Club.

'Yes,' The mobster replied.

The Old Man took the fedora off of his head and placed it on the ground. There was no longer any need for him to attempt to protect himself in any form. Darlington crouched down and brought his face close to that of the Old Man's. The two men stared into each other's eyes. Unlike any man before him, the Old Man had managed to meet David Darlington's mutilated gaze.

Darlington leaned closer to the Old Man and laughed manically.

A moment later, there was a gunshot. David Darlington stood coldly with a Colt Anaconda in hand. The power of the gun had obliterated the Old Man's face. With his last breath, he had wondered if he would be remembered. The truth was that he would, but only in nightmares.

six

THE NIGHTCLUB HAD been shut down for the night and so had The Kitano Club. It was the least that the London Mob could do to commemorate its lost leader. Within The Forge, mobsters mourned the loss of Akira Kitano undivided. Alcohol flowed frivolously as the men got drunk and shared stories.

Upstairs in the office, Darlington sat staring at his hands. There were still drops of blood of the Old Man's on him. He had avenged his brother but he still felt unfulfilled. He thought that killing the man who took away his family would fill the gaping hole within him, he had been very wrong. There was nothing more he could do. His bloodlust however continued to grow. Someone had to suffer. Someone had to pay.

There was a knock on the door. David's chubby lieutenant, Kerrington came in and settled into the seat across his Darlington. He tried to look his boss in the eye but struggled as he still wasn't wearing his hat.

'What's the situation?' Darlington asked coldly.

Kerrington took a deep breath and answered, 'Sir, the good news is that we didn't lose any men. We've got seven hospitalized from the car crashes but they're all alive and are going to survive. We also had the body taken care of and all the onlookers were generously warned that witnesses to a crime didn't usually live very long.'

'What's the bad news?'

'The police and the media. We have to arrange big payoffs for the cops to ensure that they buy the story we sell them. The media is playing us off as a threat to society and we don't need that kind of attention. We've already sent settlements to a few TV Stations and we'll take of the rest soon. All of this is going to cost us a lot of money. Even the Aviation Authority is after us. They're looking to be paid off in order to not report our helicopter flying around without a permit.'

Darlington frowned, 'Pay them all. It's worth it. We need to be strong right now and focus on uniting the two syndicates.'

Kerrington nodded with understanding and added, 'There is a still a small issue remaining, Sir. The soldiers want revenge for the death of our two men at the cinema yesterday. We've got two cops waiting downstairs with information they're willing to sell to you.'

'Send them up,' Darlington ordered.

Kerrington nodded and then rose from his seat and left the room. David considered the situation. He had torn apart the city looking for the man that had killed his brother. But to everyone else, it had seemed as though he had done so in order to avenge the leader of another syndicate. He would have to behave the same, if not more aggressively in avenging his own men. After all, their loyalty is what kept him alive.

Hult and Lomax had grown tired of waiting, especially in the company of two dozen mobsters carrying illegal weapons and wearing cheap suits. So they were thankful that the little man that seemed to be a secretary of some sort who came to escort them up for a conversation with the big boss.

The two Chief Superintendents knew a lot about David Darlington. They had studied him for quite some time when thinking about applying to the organized crime division. Fortunately, it turned out their talents were better suited to investigative work.

They had heard rumours about the man's appearance and even seen the occasional blurry picture but while they had initially chalked up what they heard to typical exaggeration, they now stood staring at a face that had been disfigured in such way that it could not be described and there was a reason no one had tried to.

'Who are you?' Darlington asked coldly.

Hult and Lomax smiled charmingly at the man with the monstrous face, with the latter deciding to do the introductions, 'I'm Chief Superintendent Lomax and this is Chief Superintendent Hult. We're from Scotland Yard's Diplomatic Affairs division.'

Darlington leaned back and asked slowly, 'Am I supposed to be impressed? Why should I care about Diplomatic Affairs?'

'You shouldn't,' retorted Lomax.

Hult carried on, 'Due to the other rather illustrious activities of your organization, the police force was stretched a bit thin today. In such a case, we were asked to come on board and help with a local investigation. We were assigned the case of the double homicide at Brix Cinema.'

'Do you know who did it?' The London Mob Boss demanded to know.

Hult and Lomax looked each other coyly. Kerrington stood in the background and watched uncomfortably as the two policemen took the situation a little too lightly.

'Well, of course we know Mr Darlington,' Hult said. 'We just wanted you to know that the individual will be brought to trial a few months from now. At that point their identity will be revealed and justice will be served.'

Lomax carried on his partner's rant, 'Of course, there is a simple way of speeding up the process...'

Darlington took a breath and played the game of the Chief Superintendents. They seemed unfazed by the gorgeous Colt Anaconda that lay on his table facing them. 'What's the process?'

'Well, Mr Darlington, you'll have to make a donation to our rather thirsty retirement fund.'

The London Mob boss was in no mood to shell out any more money, but he asked anyway, 'How much is this going to cost me?'

'Well, considering that you've prospered quite notoriously in recent years, we were thinking twenty thousand pounds. We are saving you a lot of trouble, Mr Darlington.'

Darlington leaned forward and offered a handshake. He had a much more nefarious plan in mind. Today probably wasn't the ideal day to extort the head of the London underworld and the two Chief Superintendents should've hopefully realized that.

'We have a deal.' Darlington spoke coolly as he shook Hult's hand and then Lomax's.

He then asked, 'So, who killed my men?'

Hult explained, 'Mr Darlington, your two men got quite drunk and attempted to assault two fourteen year olds—Sam Winterfield and Amy Burrows. In an attempt to defend his girlfriend, young Sam knocked your men to the ground and then used one of their guns to kill them before they could recover.'

Hult and Lomax leaned back in their chairs and smiled. They had done their bit and now they simply had to wait for the cash to arrive. Instead, Darlington picked up his Colt Anaconda and fired two rounds.

The first bullet went through Hult's neck and sent his body hurtling back. The second round hit Lomax in the skull and completely blew apart a part of his face. It probably hadn't been the best idea to fire his gun in his small metal office; the loud shots hurt Darlington's ears and it would take quite some time to get rid of the bodies, remove the bloodstains and air out the room of the stench.

Kerrington had watched the whole scene with horror. The raw unpredictability of the situation had been quite alarming. The little man looked at his boss and wondered if he had finally snapped.

seven

The darkness of the night had taken over the sky. Stars were scarce and the city was quiet. The wind blew roughly; it was probably the coldest day in July. The mansion stood tall, out of place as it had always been.

The white BMW 720 pulled up to the house and David Darlington got out. He had driven the car himself and had strictly told Kerrington to make sure that no one followed him. There were some things that were better dealt with without the interference of trigger-happy, sadistic henchmen.

Darlington wore his fedora. It had been one of the more difficult days of his life and he wasn't sure if he was happy or not standing at the end of it. He suffered from guilt. He had been through enough in his life already that he would have rather he had died than his brother. To him, Akira would always be the smarter one. He would've probably done a much better job uniting the London mob. None of that mattered now. The great responsibility had been thrust upon him and he will have to bear it alone.

The man continued to stand and simply stare at Winterfield Mansion, unsure of how to approach the situation. The Colt Anaconda sat peacefully in his coat with a brand new clip.

Darlington couldn't help but chuckle at himself as he looked around and found himself to be jealous of the Winterfield car collection. He however realized that the boy suffered from a curse of his own. He couldn't appreciate what he had and that made it so that it simply wasn't as nice to have it.

There was pressure on the man with the monstrous face. He considered his range of options but realized that there was only one way of going about things that would end in a satisfactory manner. David Darlington had done well in realizing that sometimes it wasn't about pleasing everyone or feeding a personal need for justice and peace, it was about forging the right kind of moment and treasuring it.

Darlington pulled the fedora low over his face and walked into the mansion and up the stairs leading to the door. He knocked softly on the wood. A few seconds later, the door swung open and Victor gasped with fear when he realized who had come to visit.

The door to the mansion led straight into the living room where Michael, Amy, Sam and Victor had been watching *Kill Bill* on the television. Answering the door, Victor had instantly shuffled back and reached for the gun in his waistband.

Sam looked at Darlington and then at Victor and said, 'There's no need for that. If he wanted us dead, we'd be in the ground already.'

Amy looked at Sam with fear as he said those grave words.

Darlington did his best to cover his face as he asked Sam, 'May I come in?'

'Of course,' Sam answered quickly.

Amy saw a glimpse of the visitor's face from beneath his hat and shuddered with fear.

'Michael, Victor, please take Amy upstairs. I'd like to speak with Mr Darlington alone.'

Michael instantly grabbed his daughter and quickly escorted her upstairs. But Victor didn't like the idea of leaving the young boy alone with the disfigured man. The news reporters hadn't been allowed to say anything as it was just speculation and circumstance but the tabloids had run wild with the story of the London Mob boss executing a man in the middle of a road in broad daylight.

Sam led Darlington to his father's study room where they sat on either side of a desk. It was just the way the older man had hoped they would settle down.

Darlington took his fedora off and placed it on the table. Sam stared at the monstrous face without the slightest bit of fear. There was something about the way the two were around each other that made Sam feel as though Darlington would never hurt him.

'It's been an eventful day for you, hasn't it?' Sam asked.

'You have no idea,' he answered with a smile.

Darlington simply stared at the fourteen year old across him. He wanted to try and understand what he felt for the boy but it was inexplicable. It was as though he had known him his whole life even though they'd only met once before.

'You owe me an apology Sam,' Darlington said a bit more seriously.

'What for?'

'The two men last night. They worked for me,' Darlington explained.

'Are you going to kill me?' he asked innocently.

'Not at all.'

Sam was curious, 'Why not?'

'Because you're more important than that,' Darlington spoke warmly.

Those were not the words that the boy had expected. He didn't say anything in return.

Darlington explained in a soft tone, 'When my parents were killed, I was ten. The same as you. But at the age of eighteen, my brother and I went to the home of the person that ordered their death and killed him. He was an old man that went by the name of Thompson and I still remember putting my revolver in his mouth on my eighteenth birthday and pulling the trigger.'

Sam took in the information and asked as politely as he could, 'Why are you telling me this?'

Darlington looked at the boy and explained, 'Because the man I killed today was the man that killed your parents.'

Sam leaned back in his chair. He was overwhelmed and distort. He could feel nothing more than absolute warmth. The man with the monstrous face that sat across from him had done for him what no one else could. He had helped him fulfil his lust for retribution.

The London Mob boss looked at the boy and instantly knew that they were two sides of the same coin. They were of the same fibre and being, just a generation apart. It was time for him to depart. Sam walked the man to the door and couldn't help but continue to feel strange and satiated.

Darlington strode out of the mansion but just before Sam closed the door behind him, he turned back and said to the boy, 'Remember kid, if you ever need a place to go, I've got an empire waiting for you out there.'